mountain
charm

Sydney Logan

Dedication

To Allison,
Thank you for letting me borrow your name, even if you can't read my books until you're a teenager. Thank you for being my youngest and sweetest fan.

Dedication

Table of Contents

Sydney Logan

Prologue

Angelina Clark gazed down at the shining candle. Its yellow flame flickered and glistened against the darkness of the living room. She had eagerly anticipated this day—her thirteenth birthday—since she'd been a little girl.

"Today is a special day," her mother said, her voice solemn.

Growing up, Angelina had heard the legend that had been passed down from her grandmother. It was a fairy tale—much like Cinderella, but without the glass slipper or the wicked stepsisters. Instead, this story involved nothing but a shimmering candle and a simple song, both of which would allow the young girl to blossom into a strong and intelligent young woman. She would be beautiful and—at the age of twenty-one—would find her true love.

It couldn't be a fairy tale without true love.

Angelina had always been a skeptical child and wondered if there was any truth to the story, but she had never been able to ignore the evidence. With long black hair and piercing blue eyes, her mother was stunning. Celia Clark was joyful, gifted, and wise, and her husband loved her as much today as he had on the day they'd married.

"Are you ready?" Celia asked.

Angelina nodded. Her heart was thundering, and her hands were trembling, but her mother assured her this was to be expected. The ceremony was an important rite of passage in a daughter's life—a sacred ritual that had been passed down from her ancestors. One day, Angelina would sit on the floor with her own daughter, and her daughter's candle.

"I'm ready," Angelina said, her voice brave.

Her mother smiled proudly at her daughter as they joined hands. Between them, the candle danced, casting shadows upon the walls. Angelina closed her eyes, took a deep breath, and began to sing.

"True love and sweet whispers
Till death do us part;
Send someone to love
My Appalachian heart."

Celia gave her daughter's hand a reassuring squeeze. With her eyes still tightly closed, the young girl swiftly blew out the yellow flame.

One

The crimson sky was aglow along the horizon of the Smoky Mountains. Standing on the front porch with her dog by her side, Angelina had to shield her eyes from the brilliant glare as she stared at the natural beauty of the dawn. To her, it was just another pretty daybreak, but to her mountain mama, a red sunrise was a sure sign of rain.

I'll need to remember my umbrella.

She inhaled deeply, letting the smell of the pines wash over her. So many times, Angelina had been tempted to move closer to town. After all, she was twenty-one years old, and none of her friends still lived at home.

Then again, none of her friends had a view like this from their front porch.

"Isn't it pretty, boy?" Angelina murmured, stroking the dog's coat. Cash, her faithful chocolate Lab, had been her constant companion since her tenth birthday. Fiercely protective and devoted, he always joined Angelina on her morning walks.

It was still early, and the fog had yet to lift. The sun was trying its best, but mountain mist was stubborn, and sometimes it was mid-morning before it finally disappeared. Angelina loved the haze, because it always dissipated, revealing the gorgeous green of spring and summer, or the pretty mosaic of auburn leaves in the fall. In the winter, blinding white snow covered the mountaintops and clung to the trees.

All of it was beautiful.

All of it was home.

"Angelina, breakfast is ready," her mother called from the kitchen.

Just like that, Angelina's peaceful morning was gone. Her mom's exhausted tone served as a grim reminder that not everything could be beautiful all the time.

Celia Clark's voice was always laced with a determined energy as she tried to remain strong for her daughter, but Angelina knew better. It had been nearly two years since her mother had buried the love of her life, and as much as Angelina missed her father, she knew her mom missed her husband even more.

"Come on, boy," Angelina said, tugging the dog's collar. Squaring her shoulders, she took another lingering look at the mountains before heading inside. The house smelled of bacon, eggs, and buttermilk biscuits. Angelina's stomach growled as she and Cash made their way into the kitchen.

"Morning, Mom."

Celia looked up from the frying pan and offered her daughter a smile. "Good morning, Angelina."

"How are you feeling today?"

"Oh, it's a good day. Hungry?"

They took their seats at the table, and Celia handed her daughter a glass of juice while trying to disguise her tired smile. Celia Clark might have been the strongest woman Angelina had ever known, but she was a terrible liar.

"Busy day at the shop?"

Angelina nodded and swallowed her eggs. "The Massey brothers are dropping off some of their instruments today. They've built some beautiful mandolins and fiddles."

Celia's Strings was a little music store in the foothills of the Smokies. Samuel and Celia Clark had always loved music and wanted to offer a place for local artists to sell their instruments. Angelina had worked in the shop since she'd been old enough to count change.

Celia gazed out the kitchen window. "We always need more mandolins. They sell so quickly."

Her breakfast remained untouched, but Angelina pretended not to notice. Instead, they talked about the store. Her mother always listened intently, but Celia's desire to run the shop had died along with her husband. She'd been ecstatic when Angelina had offered to manage it herself.

"Happy birthday, Angelina."

Angelina sighed. She supposed it had been too much to hope that her mom had forgotten today's date.

"Twenty-one years old. What a wonderful year you're going to have. I only hope . . ."

Celia's voice trailed off, making her daughter's heart ache. Her mom was doing that more and more—talking about the future and how she might not be around to see it.

Angelina shook her head. "I think this year is going to be just like all the others. You know I don't believe in that old spell."

Angelina had stopped believing in Appalachian magic long ago. If wishing made it so, her dad would still be alive, and her mom's hair wouldn't be falling out in the shower each morning.

Angelina Clark was officially a skeptic.

"You will," her mother murmured.

It was hard to argue with her. Despite Celia's failing health, her visions of the future were as clear as ever.

After finishing breakfast and clearing the dishes, Angelina grabbed her bag, and her mom followed her to the door. It was a half-hour drive into town, and Angelina wanted to beat the city traffic and do some paperwork before the shop opened at nine.

Celia handed her daughter an umbrella. "Red dawn. Rain's coming."

"I know."

"See? You *do* believe." Celia's blue eyes twinkled, and Angelina smiled because it was so good to see her mom excited about something. Celia reached for her daughter's blouse and adjusted the collar that didn't need adjusting at all. "You look so pretty today. I've always loved this color on you. It brings out the blue in your eyes."

All of their female ancestors had bright blue eyes. It was the one physical trait that never seemed to skip a generation.

"You have been given such gifts, Angelina. You should use them. And I wish you could see the spell as a blessing instead of a curse."

"But it *is* a curse."

Her mother laughed lightly, knowing it was a losing battle. They'd had this same argument for years. She'd always believed *curse* gave the whole thing a negative connotation. She preferred *spell* or *enchantment*, while Angelina preferred to forget she'd ever blown out that silly candle.

"My sweet, pessimistic daughter. You'll see."

Angelina grinned and kissed her mom's cheek.

"That's what you keep telling me," she said.

Soft bluegrass music flowed from the speakers, flooding the shop with the sounds of acoustic guitars and gentle mandolins. Angelina spent the morning hanging the new instruments on the far wall of the shop. They were well-crafted and beautiful, just as the Massey brothers had promised.

"Celia's right, you know," Maddie said.

Angelina shook her head and climbed down from the stepladder, taking a second to admire the craftsmanship of the newest selection of instruments. Customers flew in from as far away as California to buy them—a fact that had always made Samuel Clark immensely proud. Providing musicians with quality instruments was the one family tradition Angelina was determined to uphold.

Her best friend and business partner, however, was always reminding Angelina of the traditions she wished to forget.

They'd been best friends since elementary school, so Maddie Price knew all about Angelina's family heritage. Actually, the entire community knew. For Angelina, it hadn't been easy growing up in

Maple Ridge when the whole town believed she dabbled in witchcraft. That was why she'd always been cautious and reserved when it came to using her gifts.

Sure, she'd had some fun with it back in school. Back in eighth grade—after catching Christine Williams kissing Maddie's boyfriend in the school library—Angelina had pretended to curse Christy with pimples. It'd been a complete coincidence, of course, when the girl woke up the next day with her very first zit—right on the tip of her nose. Celia had grounded her daughter for two weeks, but even at the age of twelve, Angelina knew the punishment was worth it.

The witchcraft rumors had quieted down over the years, but some of the older residents still loved to talk about Abigail Rose, the famous Witch Doctor of Maple Ridge. If the tales were true, Angelina's great-great-great grandmother had delivered all the babies in the county and used mountain medicine to heal everything from snakebites to chicken pox.

Maddie had always been fascinated by it all and had spent most of her childhood begging Angelina's parents to adopt her.

"You are blessed, Angelina, no doubt about it," Maddie told her friend. "You are beautiful and smart. You own a successful business, and this is the year you'll finally meet the love of your life. No more horrible dates with complete losers. It's the ultimate fairy tale, and I'm a little disappointed you aren't sufficiently excited about this."

"First of all, beauty is in the eye of the

beholder," Angelina said as she walked back toward the counter. "If I *were* beautiful—which I'm not—it would be because of my mother's genes and not some crazy curse. If I am successful, it's because I work my ass off seven days a week."

Maddie laughed. "And when your true love walks through the door? Are you going to tell me it's some cosmic coincidence and has nothing to do with that spell?"

"I never should have told you that story."

"Oh, I love that story," Maddie said, her voice wistful and soft. "It's so romantic, and yet you refuse to believe it. Why wouldn't you *want* to believe it?"

Maddie sighed and twirled a lock of her curly red hair around her finger. Angelina couldn't help but think her best friend, with her ivory skin and bright hazel eyes, was the truly beautiful one. Freckles dotted her nose, despite her useless attempts over the years to conceal them with the most expensive make-up on the planet.

"For argument's sake," Angelina said, "let's say my true love walks through the door any minute now. Why would I want to be with someone if the only reason they love me is because of some ancient mountain spell my ancestors conjured centuries ago?"

From her perch on top of the counter, Maddie looked at her friend with bewildered eyes. "Angelina, I remember your thirteenth birthday party. We had strawberry cupcakes and danced to Britney Spears, and all you could talk about was that sacred candle. You were so innocent and hopeful and—"

"The word you're looking for is *naïve.*"

Maddie grinned. "I was so jealous. That candle was going to give you happiness, beauty, and love, and you believed it with all your heart. I know your faith in magic has really been shaken, but *this* is a good thing. You should believe in this."

Just then, a tall, middle-aged man walked through the door, gave the girls a nod, and headed straight for the vintage vinyl. Maddie wiggled her eyebrows, and Angelina stifled a giggle.

"If we have to play this game, could we at least hope he was born in my decade?" Angelina muttered under her breath.

Maddie nodded and hopped off the counter.

"This conversation isn't over, but I'm going to run next door and get us some coffee."

"I'd like a tea instead, and take an umbrella."

"Why?" Maddie curiously glanced out the window.

"Just take it." Angelina grabbed her mom's umbrella from behind the counter and tossed it in her friend's direction.

Maddie's eyes flickered with understanding. "I bet that was a pretty red sunrise."

"It always is."

"You know," she said, leaning her elbows against the glass counter and grinning. "You can't pick and choose, Angelina. You either believe or you don't."

It wasn't the first time she'd been called a hypocrite. Angelina was immune to it.

With a grin, Angelina nodded toward the window. In a matter of seconds, the heavens had opened.

"Maddie, I can believe in the rain. I can *see* the rain."

"I wonder what we'll *see* today." Maddie's eyes widened. "I can't leave! What if *he* shows up while I'm out getting your tea?"

With a groan, Angelina walked around the counter and grabbed her friend by the arm, all but shoving her out into the torrential downpour.

The rain continued throughout the day, keeping the customers away. Angelina was secretly glad. Even though it wasn't good for business, she couldn't deny the strange sense of satisfaction in seeing the miserable look on Maddie's face. Whenever the door would chime with an occasional customer, Maddie would practically jump over the counter to get a better look. She'd nearly given David Murray a heart attack, which wouldn't have been good considering he was still recovering from his last one.

"What can we do for you, Mr. Murray?" Angelina asked.

A disgruntled Maddie shot her a glare and headed toward the stock room.

Thank goodness it's nearly closing time.

"Evening, Angelina. I need some banjo strings."

She nodded and gingerly took the man's arm, leading him over to the selection of strings. Time hadn't been good to David. As if the heart attack wasn't enough, he was almost blind due to the cataract in his left eye. Regardless, he still drove around town and played the banjo like a pro.

His voice was low as they walked back toward the register. "Angelina, I don't mean to stick my nose where it doesn't belong, but I was just having supper over at Sally's Diner. There was some reporter snoopin' around, asking questions about your family. Said he was doing a story about Appalachian folklore and someone in Cumberland County pointed him in this direction."

It wasn't the first time a stranger had been interested in her family's history, but the attention always made her uncomfortable.

"I appreciate you telling me," Angelina said as she placed his receipt in the bag. "Did you get his name?"

"No, just that he worked for some magazine in Nashville."

She smiled and handed him his strings. "Well, I'll keep my eyes open. Thanks for letting me know."

"Sure thing." David's expression turned somber. "How is Celia feeling? I haven't talked to her in a few days."

"She's hanging in there. The treatments are hard on her."

"And on you."

Angelina nodded slowly and swallowed down the emotion that threatened to choke her.

"Don't you worry about that reporter," David said, patting her hand. "The people in Maple Ridge might be nosy, but we protect our own."

She thanked him and grabbed an umbrella. After walking David to his car, Angelina headed back inside and locked the door. When she turned around, she was met with the steely glare of her best friend.

"Why are you looking at me like that?"

Maddie's hands were on her hips. "It's closing time!"

"And I couldn't be happier. You've been so preoccupied with the spell you haven't even wished me a happy birthday."

She narrowed her hazel eyes.

"Happy birthday, you skeptic."

Angelina laughed and began to empty the register. With the day's slow sales, doing the evening bookkeeping would be a breeze.

"You have to believe in true love," Maddie said as she followed her partner back to the office, "otherwise, he'll never show up."

Angelina sighed and sat down behind the desk. "First of all, the spell doesn't stipulate he'll arrive *today*."

"I know, but your parents met on Celia's twenty-first birthday."

"Yes, but my grandmother met my grandfather almost a year after she turned twenty-one. It's not time-specific, Maddie."

"You mean I might have to wait a whole *year?*"

Angelina smirked. "My deepest apologizes. And for your information, I do believe in true love. My parents were proof that it exists. I just don't believe blowing out a candle and singing some silly song on my thirteenth birthday is going to make the man of my dreams appear out of thin air to sweep me off my feet."

"He's out there somewhere," Maddie said,

sighing dejectedly, as if it were *her* heart on the line. "What are you doing tonight?"

"Mom wanted to bake me a cake, so I'm headed home."

She frowned. "You'll never meet him at *home*, Angelina."

"Who knows, Maddie. Maybe he's waiting for me on my front porch."

"Do you promise to call me if he is?"

Her eyes were wide, and she sounded desperately hopeful, so Angelina resisted the urge to laugh at the silliness of it all. Instead, she made a vow to her best friend.

"Absolutely, Maddie. If there's a man waiting for me on my front porch, you'll be the first person I'll call."

It was dusk by the time Angelina drove out of town and up the winding mountain road that would lead her home. The sky was a pinkish-orange as the sunset lingered just above the trees. Rain was still falling, but it was nothing more than a light shower as it gently tapped against the windshield.

Angelina couldn't wait to get home. She wanted to curl up on the couch, eat a slice of birthday cake, and forget all about the curse.

By the time she reached the house, the rain had all but diminished. The fog was still dense, but it wasn't so thick that she couldn't see the black SUV parked in her mother's driveway.

Or the man sitting on her front porch.

⌒Two

There are moments in a person's life that absolutely shake them to their core. Moments that make them re-evaluate their every thought, their every decision.

This was Angelina's moment.

And she couldn't muster the courage to step out of the car.

Instead, she flexed her trembling fingers around the steering wheel and tried to comprehend the scene right before her disbelieving eyes.

There was a man on her porch.

Even through the fog, she could tell he was a handsome man.

And she couldn't be sure, but he appeared to be around her age.

A man born in her decade.

A dazed Angelina glanced ahead, and through the mist, she took a long look at the black vehicle parked in her spot.

With Davidson County plates.

Nashville.

In an instant, the moment was shattered. Her short-lived astonishment gave way to something far more familiar—something bitter and suspicious and just downright *pissed.*

Feeling ridiculous, Angelina furiously slammed her car door and stalked toward the porch. This wasn't her true love. Not at all. This was that snooping reporter from Nashville, and he was at her house, on her porch.

And petting *her* dog.

The man's eyes widened as she approached, and by the time she reached the steps, he was already on his feet. Cash, traitor that he was, gave an unenthusiastic bark and rushed to Angelina's side.

"Who the hell do you think you are?"

The man looked a little stunned.

"I'm Dylan Thomas." His eyes were a deep brown and his voice was kind. Thanks to her rage, both features were fairly easy for Angelina to ignore. "You must be Celia's daughter. Wow, I heard you were beautiful, but—"

"Dylan Thomas?" Angelina muttered coldly, interrupting his compliment. "What kind of person names their kid after some drunken Welsh poet?"

"I don't know. Maybe the same kind of person who names their dog after their favorite country music singer."

Angelina's eyes narrowed.

"Oh, Angelina, you're home!" Celia's voice cut through the tension as she carried a tray out onto the porch. "I was just getting Mr. Thomas a slice of your cake."

"Mrs. Clark, please. I've asked you to call me Dylan."

He smiled at the woman before sitting back down in the rocking chair with his plate.

Cash seemed torn, looking between the stranger and his owner, before finally releasing a resigned whine and plopping down at Angelina's feet.

The man has charmed both my mother and my dog.

"Dylan has driven all the way from Nashville to meet us," Celia said.

"*Dylan* is here to write a story about our family. Did he tell you that? Did he tell you he's been all over town, asking questions about us?"

"He mentioned it, yes." Celia smiled at the man before turning her attention back to her daughter. "You know, it's getting a bit chilly. I think I'll go find a good book and crawl into my warm bed. Give you two the chance to get acquainted."

"Mom . . ."

Celia's eyes danced with happiness, and it tugged at Angelina's heart. There was no mistaking the hope there.

Stupid spell.

"Happy birthday, Angelina."

Dylan leapt to his feet, thanking Celia again for the cake and holding the screen door open as they said good night. Angelina had to admit the man was good. Those intrinsic good manners were going to charm the pants off many of the women he would encounter throughout his life.

But not her.

"It's your birthday?"

"Yes, and it was blissfully uneventful until you showed up."

"Beautiful *and* infuriating," Dylan muttered. "Look,

Angelina, I was just given this assignment yesterday. I don't have a clue about Appalachian magic tricks or devil worshipping or whatever it is you do up in these mountains, but I have a story to write. Just let me interview you and your mom, and I'll be back on the interstate before you can say *abracadabra*."

Instead of pointing out just how ignorant he sounded, Angelina decided what he truly needed was a strong dose of fear.

"Actually, I do have something you need to see. A family heirloom. Wait here?"

Excited for any useful information, Dylan's eyes lit up and he nodded enthusiastically. Once again, those good manners kicked in, and Dylan opened the door for her.

Angelina raced inside the house. She hadn't touched it in years, but she still remembered where her father kept the key to the case. She grabbed what she needed and quickly made her way back out to the porch, letting the screen door slam behind her.

Dylan jumped out of his chair. "What the hell?"

Angelina lifted the rifle and pointed it straight at him. He didn't need to know the safety was on—or that the chamber was empty.

"This is a Remington, passed down from my father and his father, also known as an Appalachian magic wand. Just watch. It's going to make you disappear."

Angelina thought it was almost comical, hearing him curse and watching him leap off the porch. All the commotion caused her dog to chase after him, which only made Dylan sprint faster until he reached the sanctuary of his vehicle.

"Are you insane?" Dylan yelled.

"I tend to get a little crazy when someone trespasses on my property. Leave my family alone and don't come back!"

He slammed the door and had to do some fancy maneuvering to get around her car, but within seconds, the only sounds Angelina could hear were Dylan's squealing tires, Cash's noisy bark, and her mother's hearty laughter.

Dylan Thomas couldn't believe his luck.

He should have been white-water rafting down the Mississippi. *That* had been his assignment until yesterday, when his editor handed him driving directions to Maple Ridge, Tennessee, to do a feature on Appalachian witchcraft.

He was being punished. He was sure of it.

It wasn't as if the mountains weren't pretty. With his trusty camera strapped around his neck, Dylan had taken some beautiful shots today. He'd even snapped a few with his phone and sent them to his mom back in Nashville. The country was gorgeous, but to live there for any extended period of time would require plenty of alcohol and quite possibly, a lobotomy.

Throughout the day, he'd heard nothing but wonderful things about the Clarks. The mom was a sweetheart, no doubt, but the daughter ...

Well, the daughter was batshit crazy.

And beautiful. Really beautiful, with gorgeous blue eyes that seemed to flash with fire. With her long black hair and fiery temper, his attraction had hit him like a cannonball. In that split second, he'd wondered what it would feel like to hold her. To kiss her.

But then the pretty was replaced with the crazy, and

she'd chased him off the porch with a shotgun.

He wasn't going to stand for it. He had an article to write. A job to do. And he'd be damned if some redneck witch was going to cost him this assignment.

Even if she was, without a doubt, the most beautiful woman he'd ever seen.

"You didn't call me."

As in most small towns, word spread fast in Maple Ridge, and the news that Angelina Clark had chased the snooping reporter off her porch with her daddy's rifle had caused more than a few chuckles in town.

Maddie, however, wasn't laughing.

"You promised, Angelina."

"I know. I've apologized repeatedly. I just didn't think it was a big deal."

That was a lie. Angelina *knew* it would be a big deal to her best friend, which was precisely why she hadn't called. Interestingly enough, Celia hadn't said a word about Dylan over breakfast. But she was still laughing—louder than she'd laughed in years. In Angelina's mind, dealing with the irritating man had been worth the aggravation for that reason alone.

She'd missed her mother's laughter.

Maddie sighed. "You are exhausting! Was he cute?"

Angelina rolled her eyes and continued dusting the glass case that housed their collection of capos and picks. She mentally noted she'd need to order more before the end of the week.

"Ang, you have to give me *something*."

"Fine! I suppose, if forced, I'd call him handsome."

Maddie arched an eyebrow. "You suppose?"

Angelina nodded.

"Don't get too excited there."

"It's a little hard to get excited when the man is an ignorant ass."

Maddie's grin was mischievous. "That's why he's coming to you. He needs to be educated."

"Well, I'm not a teacher. He's going to have to get educated elsewhere." Her dusting complete, Angelina grabbed her cup of tea from the register and headed toward the office. "Now, if you're done with the interrogation, I need to make an order."

"If only you took your love life as seriously as you take this store!" Maddie yelled, but Angelina ignored her friend and kicked the office door shut behind her.

To Angelina's great relief, her partner left her alone, giving her the chance to spend a couple of hours getting caught up on paperwork. She finished the weekly order, worked on some monthly billing statements, and before she knew it, two hours had passed and it was time for lunch. On cue, Angelina's cell phone vibrated on her desk. Certain it was Maddie asking for her lunch order, she glanced down at the screen. It *was* from her best friend, but the text message had nothing to do with food.

**You are such a liar. He is gorgeous.
Dark hair, beautiful brown eyes, and looks so good
standing at the register.**

Angelina had never considered carrying a weapon on a daily basis, but right at this moment, she really missed her dad's rifle.

With an irritated groan, she rose from her desk and

flung open the office door. Hurrying to the front of the store, she stopped abruptly when she noticed two men standing at the register.

One was Dylan Thomas, and the other was the county sheriff.

Angelina glanced at Maddie, who was standing behind the counter with an enormous smile on her face.

Maddie had always loved drama.

After a quick glimpse around the store to make sure they were alone, Angelina squared her shoulders and looked Dylan Thomas straight in the eye.

"Get the hell out of my shop."

Dylan spun toward the sheriff.

"See? She's rude, *and* she pulled a gun on me last night. Surely that's a punishable offense."

Angelina grinned at the officer.

"How are you doing, Jack?"

"Oh, can't complain."

Jack Prescott was biting his lip to keep from laughing. It was a habit Angelina had found cute during those three months they'd dated back in high school.

"You sure caused a commotion last night, didn't you?"

"You know me, Jack. I'm protective of the things I love. My mom, my house, my dog—"

Dylan snorted. "It really pisses you off that your dog likes me, doesn't it?"

"You have *no* idea."

Maddie giggled as the two glared at each other. The sheriff maneuvered his way between them.

"Now, Angelina, you know you can't be shooting at people . . ."

Would this be a good time to admit the gun wasn't loaded?

"I didn't shoot. I just . . . pointed it at him."

Dylan muttered something about crazy hillbillies, which the sheriff ignored.

"Angelina, I talked to Celia this morning, and it seems she's not opposed to Mr. Thomas writing his story. She made it very clear to me she wants you to cooperate with him."

Dylan's smile was smug.

"Don't we all," Maddie said, her voice far breathier than usual as her eyes ghosted over Dylan's muscular frame.

Angelina groaned.

I am surrounded by traitors.

Jack gingerly touched her shoulder. "We both know your mama doesn't need any extra stress right now. Maybe this will be good for her. It'll give her something to focus on besides the chemo, you know?"

Dylan's conceited grin was gone in an instant. "Chemo?"

Jack offered Angelina a sympathetic smile just as three girls walked into the store. The teenagers were giggly as they made their way over to the CD collection.

"No more guns," the sheriff said quietly.

Too emotional to reply, Angelina nodded and left them standing there while she helped her customers.

"Dylan's like a lovesick puppy," Maddie said. "He's just sitting next to the window, pretending to play with his phone, sneaking glances at you when he thinks you aren't looking."

"I'm *not* looking."

"I know, and I don't understand that at all. How can you *not* look at the man? So what if he was a little bit of a jerk? He's from the city. He's completely out of his element, and you have no valid reason for hating him except you're scared to death his arrival proves the spell is legit."

"No, I hate him because he showed up at my house after spending the day digging for dirt on me and my family."

"That's what reporters do."

"Whose side are you on?" Angelina asked a little too loudly. Dylan's head popped up, only to drop once again as he continued to scroll through his phone.

"Yours, always. Just talk to him, Ang."

Angelina sighed. Maybe her friend was right. After all, the quicker he got his story, the quicker he'd be out of her life for good.

"The spell is not legit," Angelina mumbled. "And even if it is, *he* is not my true love, Maddie. He just can't be."

Maddie laughed quietly. "Oh ye of little magical faith. I haven't seen you that fired up in a long time. Sparks were *flying*."

"That wasn't sparks. That was intense rage."

A customer asked for help with a fiddle, and Maddie promised she'd be right with him.

"It was good to get a glimpse of the old Angelina Clark. I've missed her. Now go talk to him and put him out of his misery."

Maddie went to help the customer while Angelina tried to gather the nerve to go talk to the nosy reporter. Dylan was still sitting at the table next to the window with his eyes glued to his phone. Taking a couple of deep breaths, Angelina slowly walked toward him. He looked up, gave her a guilty smile, and shoved his phone into his pocket.

"Hey."

"Hi." Angelina glanced over her shoulder and found Maddie smiling in encouragement. Shaking her head, she turned her attention back to the infuriating man. "I was wondering if you were hungry."

Dylan looked surprised. "Hungry?"

Angelina nodded. "I thought we could grab something to eat at the coffee shop next door. They have great sandwiches and the best tea in Maple Ridge—if you like tea. If not they have coffee or soft drinks or . . ."

She was rambling, but he was staring up at her with those brown eyes, and for some reason, they were deeper and darker in the daylight.

Dylan smiled and quickly jumped to his feet.

"Lunch sounds great," he said.

Three

Dylan couldn't believe she'd invited him to lunch. He knew it was nothing more than a peace offering at her best friend's insistence, but he'd gladly take it.

The weather was nice, so they chose a table out on the sidewalk. Dylan ordered a turkey club while she chose the roast beef. They didn't say a word throughout most of the meal, but more than once, he caught himself watching her. Everything about her fascinated him, and it had nothing to do with the fact that she was supposedly a witch. It was the subtle things. Like the passion in her eyes when she was angry, or the shape of her ass in those jeans.

"You look a little dazed," Angelina muttered.

I am.

"And you're staring."

Dylan cleared this throat. "Sorry."

Before long, the food was gone, and there was nothing else to do but talk.

Angelina sighed. "Listen, Dylan. I'm sorry about the

gun."

She actually sounded sincere, so he decided to play nice, too.

"I'm sorry for showing up unannounced."

"It wasn't loaded," Angelina said, much to his surprise. "I don't know what came over me. I'm not sure if you've noticed, but I have a bit of a temper."

He grinned. "Oh, I've noticed."

Angelina fidgeted uncomfortably and gazed out at the street. Dylan knew he had to gain her trust if he had any hopes of getting his article written. He wasn't good at chitchat, but he needed to keep her talking.

"Did you always want to work in a music shop?"

"Not always. Growing up, I wanted to be a doctor."

"Oh?" That wasn't what he'd been expecting at all. "Are you still interested in medicine?"

"No."

Her voice was firm and resolute, which assured Dylan there was a story there. However, he was smart enough to realize that now was not the time to dig too deeply.

Angelina looked at him. "What about you? Did you always want to be a journalist?"

"I always wanted to be a writer, but not necessarily for a magazine. It just kind of fell into my lap."

Actually, his journalism professor had called in a favor. Being an editor for his university newspaper hadn't opened a lot of doors for the recent college graduate. Dylan had planned to start at one of the local Nashville papers and maybe do some freelance on the side. Instead, he was writing for a lifestyle magazine called *Hidden Gems*, a publication devoted to finding Tennessee's secret treasures. The job wasn't terrible. He'd gone cave exploring in the Cumberland Plateau and visited a nature reserve in Chattanooga.

And now he was witch hunting in the Smoky Mountains.

"With a name like Dylan Thomas, how could you do anything *but* write?" Angelina asked, smiling at him.

He chuckled. "I know. My mom loves his poetry. She's a literature professor at Vandy."

"And your dad?"

"No idea. He and my mom split when I was young. I have no real memories of him, and we've never been in contact with each other."

"That must be hard for you."

Dylan shrugged. "Not really. I mean, how can you miss someone you've never known?"

"I guess that's true."

He could tell she couldn't truly relate. Family seemed very important in this little mountain town, and especially to Angelina and her mom.

"Your mom is a sweet lady," Dylan said.

"Thank you. Yes, she is."

"How long has she been sick?"

Her face paled, and he knew immediately it had been the wrong thing to ask.

Angelina balled her napkin into her fist before throwing it onto the table. "I don't want to talk about that. I don't really talk about it with anyone."

"Not even with Maddie?"

"Maddie knows the basics. It's just not something I can talk about with a stranger."

The last thing he wanted to do was upset her.

"I understand. I'm sorry."

"Thanks," Angelina said with a relieved smile. "But I will answer your questions about my family. It's not my favorite topic—and Mom knows way more than I do—but I'll tell you whatever you want to know."

He felt triumphant, but he couldn't enjoy the success. Not yet.

"We don't have to do that today," Dylan said. "We can talk about whatever you like."

"What if I don't want to talk about anything?"

"Then we can just sit here."

Angelina grinned. "You know, I'm not sure your editor will be happy you're passing up an opportunity to interrogate me. Don't reporters usually have a deadline?"

"We do, but there's a little more flexibility with a human interest article like this one. These stories take massive amounts of research and travel, so they allow time for that."

"So, what's your deadline?"

"My editor didn't really give me one." That still seemed odd to him, but he hadn't questioned it. The freedom was kind of nice. "I was actually assigned to a story that was going to send me rafting down the Mississippi River, but something changed at the last minute. Next thing I know, I'm being handed directions to Maple Ridge."

Angelina laughed. "I can't even imagine your disappointment."

"Why would I be disappointed?"

She shrugged. "I don't know. I would just assume a rafting trip would be more fun than doing witch research in the mountains."

Twenty-four hours ago, he would have agreed with

her. But now that they were actually having a civil conversation, he wasn't too bothered by the fact that he was having lunch with a pretty girl who just might happen to dabble in witchcraft.

"I'm not disappointed," Dylan said, his voice soft. "I admit, I wish you and I had met under better circumstances. You know, without the rifle pointed at my face."

They both laughed.

"But no, Angelina, I can't say I'm disappointed."

A brief looked passed between them, leaving him reaching anxiously for his phone. He was in desperate need of something to distract him from the beautiful woman sitting across the table.

Suddenly, Angelina's name was being yelled from across the street.

"Oh no," she muttered under her breath.

A tall man crossed the street and headed straight to their table.

"Friend of yours?"

She sighed heavily and forced a smile as the man approached them.

"How are you, Kyle?"

"I'm great." The guy's eyes raked over her, and Dylan's jaw tightened. "You're looking good, Angelina."

Irrational, consuming jealousy flooded Dylan's veins as the two of them talked about nothing of importance. They'd obviously known each other for years, which Dylan was learning was normal in a small town like this one.

"Angelina, you should let me take you out to dinner on Friday."

"Sorry, I have plans," she replied politely.

"What about next Friday?"

Dylan finally lost his patience. "She has plans every Friday."

It was only then that Kyle acknowledged the other person at the table.

"Who the hell are you?"

"I'm the one she has plans with on Friday."

The two men stared, sizing each other up. Dylan knew he had no right, but the man obviously couldn't take a hint.

Kyle snorted. "Seriously, Angelina?"

Angelina played along. "That's right."

"Well, if you get bored—"

"I won't."

The two men shot daggers at each other before Kyle finally walked away.

"Was that fun?" Angelina grinned.

"A little."

The two of them shared a smile.

"Thank you, Dylan."

He shrugged and felt the tension relax in his shoulders. "No problem. You didn't seem particularly interested in him."

"When I was sixteen, Kyle begged my parents for permission to take me to the movies. It was my first date, and they agreed, despite my father's misgivings. Dad was right. Kyle was far more interested in feeling me up than watching whatever was on the screen."

Jealousy wasn't an emotion that Dylan was particularly familiar with, and he couldn't understand why he was feeling it now. He barely knew this girl.

He forced a chuckle and grabbed his phone once

more.

"Are you one of those people who are forever attached to their cell?"

He fidgeted in his chair. "Yeah, I guess I am. I was . . . doing some online research."

"On me?"

"No, on your dad."

"Why would you be doing research on my dad?"

He noticed the quiver in her voice. Didn't she understand he was a reporter? Gathering facts was his job.

"I was just looking at his obituary, Angelina. I was curious."

Grabbing her tray, Angelina stood up and angrily shoved the empty containers into the trash.

"Then you ask me! You don't sit in my father's shop and read his obituary on your fancy phone. You ask *me*!"

Dylan was instantly on his feet. "I couldn't ask you. Until an hour ago, you weren't even speaking to me!"

"And now I remember why!"

Angelina slammed down her empty tray and ran back to her shop.

Few things relaxed Angelina more than sitting on her front porch. Maybe it was the rhythm of the rocking chair. Maybe it was fresh mountain air. Maybe it was the sense of security that only came from being at home. Whatever it was, she was in desperate need of calming.

She realized her anger toward Dylan and his glimpse into her dad's life was irrational. Of course he'd be interested to know why her father wasn't around. She had no idea how much her mom had told him before she'd arrived last night. Maybe she hadn't told him a thing. Any good reporter would wonder why there wasn't a father in a home where family was clearly a priority.

It had been two years since her father's death. Two long, bitter years filled with crushing disappointment and monumental heartbreak. Like most reporters, Dylan was far too curious about everything, and Angelina had a feeling that a simple explanation of 'my dad passed away after a courageous battle with cancer' wouldn't satisfy him.

Dylan would want details, and she wasn't ready to share them.

It wasn't as if her dad's cancer was different from any other. It was the same horrible, debilitating disease that affected nearly every family in one way or another. The only difference was that most patients didn't have a daughter who was supposedly gifted with the power to heal. In the end, she'd been no more capable of healing him than his Harvard-educated oncologist.

"We're having a guest for supper," Celia announced as she made her way out onto the porch. She was moving a little slowly today—a fact her daughter noticed but didn't dare mention. Her mother was stubborn in her determination to at least *appear* healthy and strong. "I thought we'd have chicken."

Angelina didn't have to ask who was coming for dinner.

"I'm sure Dylan will love it."

Celia's rocking chair creaked, but it wasn't annoying. Someday, Angelina might have to sit on the porch without her, and she'd be forced to close her eyes to remember the sound.

"Sweetheart, why are you crying?"

Angelina bowed her head and blinked away her tears.

"I'm not crying."

"You're too pure of heart to tell a believable lie." It was one of Celia's favorite expressions and had deterred her daughter from being dishonest as a child. "Your mind and spirit are conflicted today."

"My mind and spirit are conflicted every day."

A lone tear trickled down Angelina's cheek, and she quickly wiped it away.

"Angelina, you don't always have to be the strong one. Talk to me, please. Is it about Dylan?"

She nodded. "He was reading Dad's obituary today. I know it's just because he's curious, but . . ."

Celia nodded, encouraging her to continue.

"We argued. I yelled. He yelled."

Her mother chuckled.

"The two of you certainly yell a lot. There's so much passion there."

Angelina shook her head. "I know you and Maddie have this wild notion that Dylan is the love of my life, but I can assure you that's not the case. All we do is fight. He's just a nosy reporter wanting to unearth our family secrets, and since you told Jack you want me to cooperate—"

"I told Jack I would *like* for you to cooperate. The decision is yours."

"I don't understand. You've never wanted to attract this kind of attention by sharing our family's stories. Why now?"

Just then, the sound of crunching gravel echoed as Dylan's black SUV came to a stop in the driveway. Celia smiled as she watched him climb out of his vehicle.

"Angelina, you have fought so hard against what you are destined to be that you have forgotten who you are.

You are carrying a weight that isn't yours to bear. It's time to move on with your life."

Of course it's my weight to bear. I failed him. And I will fail you.

Angelina watched as her dog raced down the steps, barking and leaping happily as Dylan walked toward the house.

"You see, even Cash likes him," Celia said, laughing lightly. "I trust him, Angelina. I believe he was sent here for a purpose, and when that reason is revealed, I believe our family heritage and his magazine article will be the very last things on his mind."

"Celia, dinner was delicious," Dylan said graciously.

Angelina knew he was just being polite. Dinner had been downright painful. Despite her mother's attempts to soothe the tension, the two had remained stubborn in their resolve to ignore each other throughout the entire meal.

Celia thanked him as Angelina filled the sink with water for the dishes. Suddenly, she felt her mother's hand on her shoulder.

"It's a lovely evening, Angelina. Why don't the two of you take Cash for a walk down by the pond? I bet he'd love to see it—wouldn't you, Dylan?"

Angelina rolled her eyes at her mom's blatant attempt at matchmaking and settled the plates into the soapy water.

To her shock, Dylan was the voice of reason.

"I'm not sure that's a good idea. Angelina and I tend to have a problem whenever we try to have a conversation. It always ends in an argument."

Celia all but shoved her daughter away from the sink. "Well, that's because the two of you are just alike.

Passionate and pig-headed. Besides, you need to find a way to get along if you have any hopes of writing your article."

Angelina was stunned. Her mother was a master manipulator. Who knew?

Dylan sighed loudly and turned in her direction.

"Angelina, would you like to take a walk with me?"

Celia's bright blue eyes pierced through her daughter, silently begging her to try. Angelina nearly choked on the maternal guilt.

"Fine," she muttered.

Her mother beamed. "Wonderful! Oh, take your guitar, Angelina. And your jacket. It's always chilly by the water."

Four

Their walk to the pond was a quiet one. If it hadn't been for the birds in the trees and Cash's occasional barking at the squirrels, it would have been completely silent. Dylan and Angelina reached the tiny wooden dock, and Cash jumped into the water. They both laughed, and the tension began to fade.

"It's pretty out here."

Angelina pulled her guitar out of its case and placed it in her lap. "All of this used to belong to my grandfather. My mom and dad were very attached to this pond."

"Why's that?"

She gently strummed the guitar as she told the story.

"An old Appalachian legend says if you name a hook after the person you desire—and you catch a fish with the hook—that person is your true love. Dad was really crazy about my mom, and he was a good fisherman, so to prove his love was true, he brought her to this pond for their first date."

Dylan laughed. "And let me guess. He named a fish hook after her?"

"He did," Angelina said with a grin, "but what he didn't know was the pond was nearly empty of fish because of the drought that summer. It was my grandpa's pond, so Mom knew this, of course, but she didn't mention it to my father. She was a big believer in the legend and decided to put his love to the test."

"Did it work?"

"My dad caught the biggest catfish in the pond."

Dylan laughed. Angelina failed to mention that her parents had been introduced on her mom's twenty-first birthday. She was trying to avoid that conversation as long as she possibly could.

"So I guess it was true love," Dylan replied.

"Yes, it was."

He looked thoughtful. "What a great story. Does it make you sad to be out here?"

"No sadder than anywhere else."

Their legs dangled off the side of the wooden dock. Cash was in heaven, splashing around in the water and chasing the fish and the frogs. Angelina played the chorus of "Landslide" while Dylan hummed along.

"You like Fleetwood Mac?" she asked.

"Only the Stevie Nicks years."

"Me, too."

They grinned at each other. Angelina couldn't believe they actually had something in common.

"Your mom is subtle as a tank, isn't she?"

She laughed. "You noticed, huh?"

"She doesn't hide it very well. It seems . . . irrationally important to her that you and I get along."

"Well, there's a reason for that."

"Are you going to tell me what it is?"

"Nope."

Dylan sighed and leaned back on his palms, stretching out in the fading sunlight. Angelina couldn't deny he was handsome. He'd even worn a shirt and tie to dinner, much to her mom's delight. After a few moments, she realized she was staring. Dylan caught her eye and smirked. Embarrassed, Angelina quickly turned her attention back to her guitar.

Sitting up, he shifted a little closer to her body, brushing her arm with his. "You're really pretty when you blush, Angelina. I mean, you're always pretty, but . . ."

"Even when I'm an unreasonable bitch?"

Angelina looked up from her guitar to find Dylan's face much closer than she'd anticipated. Their eyes locked, and she felt exposed under the intensity of his stare.

"You aren't a bitch. You're just heartbroken, and I know some of that has to do with your mother's illness and your father's death. But there's more. There's so much more, isn't there?"

Tears flooded her eyes, and when one traitorous tear crept down her cheek, Dylan lifted his hand and gently brushed it away. His touch was unbelievably tender, and she didn't deserve it. She'd been so rude, and yet here he was, wiping her tears and being kind.

Sniffing quietly, Angelina placed her guitar back in its case before reaching into her jacket for the bud she always carried in her pocket.

"What's that?" Dylan asked.

"This is the bud of a balsam fir tree. Mom says they have magical qualities and supposedly mend a broken heart. I've carried it since the day my father passed away."

Dylan gazed at the blossom in her palm.

"Do you believe in magic, Angelina?"

She wrapped her fingers around the tiny bud and tossed it into the pond. They watched as the dead flower crumbled and scattered in the water.

"Not anymore," she said.

The day had been one of the most stressful of Angelina's professional life. She had spent her morning on the phone, arguing with a vendor regarding a shipment of banjos she'd received but never ordered. After dealing with that mess, she'd caught a teenager trying to steal a CD from the clearance rack. Thanks to the storm raging outside, the power had flickered on and off all afternoon. And right at closing time, a group of tourists had walked into the shop. After spending an hour looking at everything in her store, the group waltzed right out the door without purchasing so much as a guitar pick.

And she'd handled it all on her own, because her best friend was home with the flu.

Angelina had nearly made it home in the torrential downpour when she felt a vibration under her feet. The steering wheel jerked in her hand, and she groaned.

"Please don't be a flat tire," she muttered under her breath.

Angelina pulled onto the side of the two-lane road and threw her jacket's hood over her head. The rain fell in sheets while lightning flashed overhead. A quick glance at her driver's side confirmed her worst fear, and she kicked the deflated tire before climbing back into her car. Angelina had a spare in the trunk—and she knew how to change a flat—but she didn't want to attempt changing it in the middle of the storm. Soaking wet and on the verge of tears, she angrily slapped the hazard light button and turned on the radio while waiting for the monsoon to pass.

"Power outages are widespread, and trees are down throughout the county," the announcer said. "This is a dangerous storm with up to sixty mile per hour winds . . ."

Fantastic. She grabbed her cell and called to check on her mom. Celia was at a restaurant in Pigeon Forge, safe and sound and far away from the storm. While they were talking, Angelina distinctly heard the hearty laughter of a man. She was just about to ask about her mother's dinner date when a sharp rapping on the window made her scream.

"Angelina, are you all right?"

Glancing in the rearview mirror, Angelina spotted Dylan's SUV.

Of course.

"I'm fine, Mom. I'll call you later."

Angelina tossed her phone back into her bag before rolling down the window.

"Are you okay?" Dylan shouted over the rain and wind. He was absolutely soaked, despite the umbrella over his head.

"Just a flat. I'll change it when the storm passes."

"The storm isn't passing, Angelina. It's supposed to do this all night long. Let me take you home. We'll come back tomorrow and get your car."

Sighing deeply, she turned off the lights and ignition. After locking up, she quickly followed Dylan to his vehicle.

"I'm sorry about soaking your seats," she said once they were settled into the cab.

"No big deal. How long have you been sitting out here?"

"Just a few minutes. I was waiting for the storm to pass before I changed my tire."

He looked surprised. "You can do that?"

"Umm, yes?"

Dylan held up his hands. "No offense. I just don't know many girls who can."

The man was maddening, but the last thing she wanted to do was argue. She was tired and grouchy, and any conversation with him wouldn't end well.

"No offense taken," Angelina replied sweetly. "Would you mind taking me home now?"

Dylan smirked and pulled his SUV out onto the highway.

"We can't just talk like two normal human beings, can we?"

"Nope."

"I wonder why that is?"

Angelina bit her lip and stared out the windshield. The wipers flung water from side to side in a dizzying rhythm that made her eyes cross.

"So now you aren't talking to me at all?"

Angelina wondered why he would want to talk when every discussion ended in an argument. Still, he was nice enough to rescue her, so she decided to throw him a bone.

"How 'bout this weather?"

"The weather sucks, Angelina."

She shrugged. He couldn't say she didn't try.

"Not every conversation ends in a fight," Dylan pointed out. "Last night was nice."

Last night at the pond *had* been nice, but today, she

was regretting being so open and honest.

"How much of my parents' love story is going to be featured in your article?"

"None, if you don't want it to be."

That surprised her. "Really?"

"Really. I'm not a jerk, Angelina, despite what you think."

She offered him a soft, relieved smile before turning toward the window once again. The driveway was just ahead, and she couldn't wait to get out of her wet clothes and take a hot shower.

"I hope you have plenty of candles and a flashlight," Dylan said.

"Why?"

He pointed toward the dark house. Celia always left the porch light on, so it was easy to assume the electricity was out.

"Think your mom's okay?" Dylan asked as the vehicle came to a stop in the driveway.

"She's fine. She's having dinner with a friend in Pigeon Forge."

A male friend. I'll have to remember to interrogate her in the morning.

Angelina reached for the door handle. "Well, I appreciate the ride. Thanks, Dylan."

He looked hesitant. "I'm not sure how I feel about you spending the night alone, not to mention without electricity."

"I'm a big girl, and I have a huge Labrador retriever to keep me company."

Dylan shook his head. "I'm not leaving you. I'll sit out on the porch if you don't want me to come inside, but

I'm not going anywhere."

"You realize you're being ridiculous, right?"

He shrugged.

Angelina rolled her eyes. "Fine."

They climbed out of the SUV and raced through the rain toward the porch. Cash's noisy bark could be heard coming from just inside the door.

"Hey, boy," Angelina said, pushing her way past the yapping dog and unzipping her wet hoodie. Cash continued barking happily as he pounced on Dylan, who was still lingering outside. The poor animal was looking between the two of them, all torn and confused, until Angelina laughed.

"My dog is going to have a heart attack if you don't come inside."

Dylan grinned. "Are you sure?"

She pretended to give it some thought. "Are you going to attack me?"

"Only if you want me to."

Angelina felt her pulse quicken. *Is he flirting?*

"Umm . . . there are candles on the fireplace mantle," she said, hoping he didn't notice the tremor in her voice. "You know where the bathroom is, if you want to dry off. I'm going to go find a flashlight and change into something warm."

Using her cell phone light as her guide through the darkened house, Angelina located a real flashlight and extra candles in the hallway closet. Then she headed to her bedroom and changed into a pair of sweats and fuzzy socks. Dylan's clothes were wet, too, so she found one of her dad's old flannel shirts and a pair of sweatpants in the back of her mom's closet.

When she returned to the living room, four candles had been lit on the mantle of the fireplace, and Dylan and Cash were sitting on the couch.

"I thought you might like to change, too," Angelina said, handing him the shirt and sweats.

"Thanks."

He headed to the guest bathroom while she took his spot on the couch. The storm continued to rage outside, but now that she was home, the sound of the rain was relaxing as it pounded against the roof. Cash snuggled close while she got comfortable on the couch. Leaning her head back, Angelina closed her eyes and prayed for the tension in her shoulders and neck to ease now that her crappy day was over and done.

But it wasn't done, because Dylan was in her house.

And naked in her bathroom.

Dylan fumbled with the last button. It was a man's shirt, and he wondered if it belonged to an ex-boyfriend? Or maybe her father?

He hoped it had belonged to her father.

After towel-drying his hair and placing his wet clothes across the tub, he slowly made his way back into the living room. Angelina was on the couch with her head leaned back, rolling it from side-to-side. She was wearing the biggest, slouchiest sweatshirt and most ridiculous looking socks, and yet she was still the sexiest girl he'd ever seen.

He was desperate to touch her.

Clearly she'd had a rough day. Having a flat tire in the middle of a storm would stress out anyone. Giving her a neck massage would be the gentlemanly thing to do.

Right?

"I give kickass massages," he said as he stepped closer.

Cash jumped off the couch and trotted off toward the kitchen. Dylan took it as a sign of male solidarity. Thank God the dog liked him.

"I bet you do." Angelina smirked, but he couldn't help but notice the flush of her cheeks and the way it spread across her neck.

"I'm serious. Sit up."

Dylan sat down on the couch, and she sighed before turning around. He brushed her hair aside and placed his hands on her shoulders, kneading them softly. Angelina's groan vibrated through him, and he closed his eyes, willing his body to calm down.

"That feels so good."

Not helping.

Dylan chuckled. "Told you so."

"Shut up," she mumbled.

The storm raged outside, but it was easy to ignore as his hands became acquainted with her body. His fingers drifted along her spine, slowly loosening her tired muscles. Dylan moved closer, letting his chest brush against her back.

"Better?" His warm breath tickled her ear, and he smiled when she trembled beneath his touch.

"Yes."

He allowed his fingers to drift along her skin. Angelina's breath hitched when he slipped his hand beneath her sweatshirt, letting it rest briefly on the small of her back.

Her skin was so soft. And this was just a tiny bit of flesh on her back. He didn't dare imagine the rest of her.

"Cold?" Dylan's voice was a throaty whisper against her ear.

He let his fingers ghost up her spine once again, stalling when he reached the nape of her neck. He lingered there, loving the feel of her skin and wisps of her hair against his fingertips.

"Angelina—"

Suddenly the room was flooded with light.

Dylan blinked rapidly, as if he were coming out of a trance.

They both let out shaky breaths as Angelina jumped to her feet. She walked toward the fireplace and extinguished the candles before turning around again.

She looked as confused as he felt.

Dylan slowly rose from the couch. She took a step closer until the two of them were merely inches apart. He lifted his hand, cupping her cheek before letting his fingers slide down to her neck. Her pulse was pounding, and he wondered if his was just as frantic.

"Storm's gone," Angelina whispered.

He knew it was her lame attempt to laugh off whatever had just taken place between the two of them.

But Dylan knew, without a doubt, the storm was far from over.

Five

Feeling a bit more level-headed, Dylan spent the next day doing research in the Maple Ridge Public Library. The building was a little hole-in-the-wall with a sweet librarian by the name of Shirley Henry. Dylan didn't ask, but the woman had to be pushing eighty, and she was a fount of useful information.

"All of the sisters were witches," Shirley explained.

They were gathered at a table, and Dylan was leafing through a pile of local historical journals.

"How many sisters?"

"Three," the librarian said. "Abigail, Catherine, and Savannah. Of the three, Abigail was the brightest. She was very focused on her craft, especially after the *accidental* death of her husband."

Dylan noted her tone. "Accidental, huh?"

"Liver failure. Very tragic. And quick. Abigail's husband was not a nice man. You'll read all about him in this book." She pointed toward a giant leather-bound volume. "Trust me, though. He was a bastard."

Dylan smirked and grabbed his pen "Got it. So Abigail Rose would be Angelina's great-great grandmother?"

"Add one more *great*," Shirley said, and Dylan nodded as he scribbled on his legal pad. "Abigail was a witch doctor. Now, to be honest, most of her home remedies were brewed in a pot and had nothing to do with real magic, but the woman really knew her herbs. To a mountain town without a doctor for a hundred miles, Abigail Rose was an angel."

Dylan was confused. "So, if her remedies weren't magical, how do you know the sisters were actually witches?"

"The sisters all had special talents. Gifts. And those gifts were passed down from generation to generation. Some of the daughters have been telepathic. All of them are beautiful. Celia's mother was rumored to have the ability to predict the weather. She was quite popular with the farmers."

It all sounded ridiculous to him, except for the fact they were all beautiful. If Angelina were any indication, the gene pool had to have been breathtaking.

"What about Celia and Angelina? What are their gifts?"

Shirley grinned. "I'm afraid that's their story to tell."

Dylan frowned. He'd only been in Maple Ridge for a few days, but he'd learned very quickly that, while the townsfolk were more than happy to gossip about the witches of the past, none of them were eager to talk about Angelina and her mother.

After leaving the library, Dylan found himself walking

toward the music store. His body was drawn like a magnet to the place, but he couldn't seem to control it. He wanted to be near her all the time. It was the strangest feeling, being this attracted to a woman he barely knew.

But he was getting to know her.

And he liked her.

He could admit that much to himself. Yes, Angelina was gorgeous, but it was more than just her blue eyes and soft skin. He didn't see it often—because he pissed her off on a daily basis—but he knew she was sweet and kind. She loved her mother, her music store, and her dog, and she loved them passionately.

Was she a witch?

He had no idea.

But he couldn't wait to find out.

"Angelina likes to pretend she doesn't believe in magic, but we've been friends a long time, and I've seen it with my own eyes."

"What have you seen?" Dylan asked.

Angelina shook her head and continued dusting the fiddles along the back wall. She'd given Dylan permission to talk to anyone in town who'd willingly answer his questions. In exchange, he'd promised to limit his research into her father's death and Celia's illness. The people of Maple Ridge—especially the older folks—told the stories better than Angelina ever could and would be able to give him the basic information he needed for his article. Foolishly, she'd assumed Dylan would seek out the old men down at the diner or maybe flirt with Ms. Henry down at the library.

She should have known he'd want to interview the

most curious—and most talkative—one of all.

"Well," Maddie said as she hopped up on the counter, "did you know Angelina's great-great-great grandmother was a witch doctor?"

He nodded. "Abigail Rose. Her name keeps popping up in my research."

"The woman was a miracle worker," Maddie replied, her voice full of reverence for her friend's ancestor. "She delivered babies, healed the sick, cured diseases . . ."

"From what I've read, though, most of the healing was done with herbs."

Angelina smiled. He really had been doing his research.

"But it isn't *all* done with herbs," Maddie said quietly, and Angelina stiffened, because her best friend was about to reveal something very personal. "When we were in elementary school, four of us were playing basketball in the school gym. Billy Ross was dribbling toward the goal when he tripped over his own feet and broke his wrist. The kid was screaming in agony, and my best friend—my beautiful and gifted best friend—placed her hand on his wrist. *Just her hand.* The bone was healed, and Billy was back on his feet before the gym teacher could even make it across the court with a first-aid kit."

Angelina could feel Dylan's eyes on her as she stepped off the ladder. Out of all the stories Maddie could've shared, did she really have to start with *that* one?

"And there wasn't an herb in sight," she finished softly.

Customers began to shuffle inside, and Maddie welcomed them to the store while Angelina continued dusting and rearranging in preparation for the busy weekend. The Maple Ridge Music Festival always brought potential shoppers to the music store. The weekend-long event featured local music and crafts and was the town's only tourist attraction, bringing in visitors from miles around.

Throughout the rest of the busy day, Angelina had the feeling that someone was staring at her.

And to her great disappointment, it wasn't always Dylan.

The first time, it was Corey Ellis—a tall blonde who had just opened the new hardware store in town. A little later, it was Brad Tompkins, who pretended to be interested in one of her mandolins but really just wanted to ask her out to dinner. Angelina made up some excuse as to why that wasn't possible, and when he left, Brad was without a date and the mandolin still hung on her wall.

Angelina wasn't used to all this attention.

Maddie, however, was thrilled.

"That spell is really kicking in," she whispered in her friend's ear.

"Stop it."

"I'm serious. There isn't a man in this room who can keep his eyes off you, and that includes my favorite reporter from Nashville."

Angelina grinned. "Do you know many reporters from Nashville?"

"No, but even if I did, Dylan would still be my favorite."

Angelina glanced toward the window to find Dylan standing there, gazing at her. Her body still tingled from his massage, and his intense look was making her a little dizzy. Luckily the shop was crawling with people, so she didn't have time to stand around and stare at the handsome reporter with the gentle hands.

Later that afternoon, Angelina was busy showing an antique banjo to a customer from Virginia when she heard a familiar laugh that made her skin crawl. She looked up to find Adam McDonald standing next to the register, shaking hands with one of the local musicians.

Adam walked casually over to the instruments, stopping to admire one of the more expensive Gibson guitars they'd just put on display. A nervous Angelina offered the banjo to the man and walked slowly over to the counter. She took comfort in the fact that the shop was full of people, and Adam had never been one to make a scene.

Dylan noticed her agitation and was immediately by her side.

"What is it? What's wrong?"

Determined to keep her cool, Angelina began to rearrange the counter display of guitar picks. Dylan watched her every move, but it didn't make her edgy. She found it comforting, which was a little ironic considering Adam's possessive tendencies and Angelina's absolute rebellion against them.

Adam McDonald had been her first serious boyfriend. She'd rarely dated in high school, but he'd worn her down with his charming smile and all-American good looks. As captain of the basketball team, Adam had been the most popular guy in school, with girls worshiping at his feet.

For some reason, he'd picked Angelina.

At first, his controlling nature had been flattering. Friends told her it must be wonderful to have a boyfriend who truly loved her, so she'd ignored her gut instinct—and the warnings of her parents—and allowed him to dictate every second of her life. When she finally realized their relationship was far from healthy, Angelina had half-heartedly conjured a spell to banish him from her life. Naturally, it hadn't worked, and when she had tried the more traditional route of simply breaking up with him, Angelina had witnessed a side of Adam McDonald she'd never dreamed existed.

"Who is he, Angelina?" Dylan asked.

"He's an asshole who shouldn't be allowed to step one miserable foot inside this shop," Maddie muttered angrily.

"He's nobody."

"Then why are you trembling?" Dylan took her hand and squeezed it softly.

Maddie slammed the register shut just as Adam appeared.

"Good afternoon, ladies," he said, his voice laced with that same Southern drawl the girls had loved back in school. He placed the Gibson guitar on the counter and grinned, but his phony smile turned into a frown when he saw Angelina and Dylan's joined hands.

Very calmly, Angelina pulled her hand away and reached for the guitar to check the value. Normally she wouldn't make her loyal customers pay full retail price for an instrument, but Adam McDonald deserved no favors.

Maddie was livid. "Don't you dare sell him that guitar, Angelina."

Angelina breathed deeply. The last thing she wanted was for Adam to think he intimidated her in any way.

"Dylan, would you please take Maddie to lunch?"

Angelina asked, proud of her steady voice. "She gets a little grouchy when she hasn't eaten."

"I'm not leaving you." Dylan's tone was firm and resolute.

"Neither am I," Maddie said.

Adam smirked and handed Angelina his credit card.

"You're as beautiful as ever, Angelina. How are you?"

Without saying a word, she swiped his card. Maddie huffed loudly and stormed off. Dylan, however, remained rooted to his spot at Angelina's side.

"Are you looking forward to the festival?" Adam asked.

Angelina ignored his question and handed him the credit card receipt to sign. She'd never been so rude to a customer, but this wasn't just some random shopper. He didn't seem offended in the least. He simply signed his name to the slip and handed it back.

"Have a good day, Angelina."

The bastard's smirk remained on his face, even as he walked out the door with her guitar in his hand.

The cancer treatment center in Knoxville was brightly lit and decorated in soft blues and creams. It was meant to set a peaceful tone, and to the patients, it probably offered some sort of calm. For Angelina, it had the opposite effect. It did, however, make her forget all about her encounter with Adam McDonald.

Sometimes, a little perspective was all one needed.

With her banana Popsicle in hand, Celia chatted with a fellow patient while the IV pumped their bodies full of poison. The doctor had suggested something to help with the nausea, and Popsicles seemed to do the trick. They'd been lucky so far, and the treatments hadn't been too brutal on Celia's body.

"My daughter will be graduating from college in May," the woman said proudly. Her name was Teresa, and she lived with her husband just outside of Knoxville. "I can't wait to see her walk across the stage."

"That will be wonderful," Celia agreed.

Angelina heard the wistful tone of her mom's voice. While Celia had been thankful when her daughter had taken over the shop, a small part of her wished that Angelina had gone to school. She hadn't mentioned it in a while, but during the drive home, she broached the subject.

"You could still go to college, you know."

"Mom, you know how busy the shop keeps me. Besides, I've lost any desire I ever had to practice medicine."

Celia sighed. "I know your beliefs have been shaken since the death of your father, but the power to heal is such an amazing gift."

"It's only an amazing gift when it works."

Celia leaned her head back against the seat and closed her eyes. The treatments drained her, leaving her physically weak and emotionally exhausted. The hour drive back to Maple Ridge was normally a quiet one, so Angelina was a little surprised when her mom started talking again.

"I've invited Dylan to dinner tonight."

This wasn't exactly breaking news. Dylan had been a guest at their table almost every night since he'd arrived in Maple Ridge. Never had she seen her mother so willing to talk to a stranger.

"He'll have some questions for me. Maddie told him

about Billy Ross's wrist."

Celia grinned. "I bet that particular story has made Dylan even more curious about you."

"I'm sure. He also met Adam McDonald yesterday."

Celia tilted her head toward her daughter. "I thought he was living in Asheville now."

"I think he's back for the festival. Tourists have started to trickle into town. It should be a good weekend for the shop."

Angelina could feel her mother's eyes on her as she continued to drive.

"Did he upset you, Angelina?"

She shook her head, and the remaining drive home was a quiet one. They never talked about Adam, but Angelina wasn't one to keep secrets from her mother. Besides, Dylan was sure to mention him tonight, and she didn't want her mom blindsided by the news that her ex-boyfriend had made an appearance.

It was nearly dark by the time they made it back to Maple Ridge. As they pulled into the driveway, Angelina wasn't at all surprised to find Dylan's vehicle parked in her spot.

"You gave him a key?"

"Yes."

Angelina shook her head, and her mom laughed.

"What's so funny?

"You'll see," Celia said, smiling happily.

Angelina groaned and stepped out of the car. While she was thankful the cancer and chemo hadn't affected her mother's visions, it wasn't much fun being kept in the dark.

As soon as they stepped inside the house, the

undeniable aroma of garlic filled the air. A grinning Celia took her daughter by the arm and pulled her toward the kitchen, and that was where they found Dylan. He was standing next to the table, whistling and buttering garlic bread.

Angelina gasped, and his head shot up in surprise. He smiled sheepishly at the two of them before turning toward the stove. As he placed the bread inside the oven, Angelina spotted her mom's pink apron tied around his waist.

It was the funniest thing she'd ever seen.

And quite possibly the sweetest.

"Celia didn't eat much tonight."

It was almost midnight, and Dylan and Angelina were sitting on the front porch. He was in one of the rocking chairs while she sat on the step with her back pressed uncomfortably against a beam. Cash's head rested in her lap, and Angelina trailed her fingers through his fur while he snored.

"The treatments really wipe her out. I was surprised she ate anything at all."

"What kind of cancer?"

"Breast."

He nodded. "Did she have surgery?"

"Yeah, a single mastectomy. The oncologist ordered the chemo just as a precaution. We go back in a few weeks for more blood work."

"What happens then?"

Bitterness stuck in her throat, making it impossible to answer him. Cash sensed her sadness and snuggled closer, and she rapidly slid her fingers through his coat.

"Angelina, I'm sorry."

She blinked back her tears as Dylan rose from the rocker and joined her on the step. Very gently, he took her hand in his, giving it a squeeze.

"Aren't treatments expensive?"

Angelina nodded. "Dad's life insurance policy helps pay most of her medical expenses. We're very lucky."

For a few minutes, the only sounds they could hear were an owl in the distance and Cash's soft snores. When Dylan finally spoke, his voice was just a whisper.

"I read about your ancestors and their gifts. Did you really heal that boy's wrist? Just by touching him?"

Angelina nodded.

Dylan gazed at her hand as if it were some kind of science experiment. His face flickered with so many conflicting emotions.

Indecision. Disbelief. Wonder.

Understanding.

"Your touch heals, but it doesn't cure," he said softly.

Angelina nodded and closed her eyes, surrendering to the tears that were so desperate to fall.

Six

The Maple Ridge Music Festival was in full swing. Brightly decorated booths lined each side of the street as music streamed from the stage at the far end of the road. Despite its name, the festival wasn't just about music. It was an amazing display of local talent, offering everything from homemade crafts to beaded jewelry. The Morton sisters were selling their quilts and canned goods, while their husbands sold their leather wallets and belts in the neighboring booth. A customer could buy cotton candy at the Baptist church tent or burgers and fries from the high school band.

Because Celia's Strings was right in the middle of town, they never bothered to set up a booth. They simply opened the doors, and tourists could come and go as they pleased. In the one hundred years since the festival's inception, it had only been canceled once because of rain.

Dylan pointed his camera toward the street and snapped a few pictures. "This is amazing. The crowd is a little thin, though. Is that normal?"

"It's still early," Maddie said. The three of them were sitting on a wooden bench just outside the door. "Just wait. This place will be crawling with people this afternoon."

"And tonight," Angelina said with a grin.

"What's tonight?"

Maddie bounced in her seat. "The concert! At sundown, some of our local bands take the stage. The booths close and the street becomes a giant dance floor!"

"Maddie *really* loves to dance."

Dylan grinned. "What about you, Angelina? Do you love to dance?"

"It's okay."

Her best friend snorted. "She *loves* to dance. Especially slow dances."

Subtle, Maddie.

"Is Nick coming in this weekend?" Angelina asked. Maddie and Nick Phelps had been high school sweethearts. He'd been working for his dad's trucking company since graduation, and weeks would pass before he had the chance to come home.

"He'll be here this afternoon, which means I am taking the early shift at the shop while you and Dylan enjoy the festival." Maddie leapt off the bench and followed a couple of customers inside. "Make sure he tries Ms. Imogene's blueberry dumplings!"

Angelina sighed loudly, causing Dylan to chuckle. He grinned and jumped to his feet.

"Come on, Angelina. Take me to the dumpling booth."

"Then there was Camilla Jones—one of my distant cousins who lived in Maple Ridge way back in 1840. She was born at midnight, which according to mountain tradition means she had the ability to talk to spirits. Camilla loved talking to the ghosts of Civil War soldiers."

Dylan polished off his third bowl while Imogene Williams shared her family's stories. Angelina had rolled her eyes throughout most of the conversation, but at least the dumplings were good.

Imogene wiped her hands on her apron and smiled at the two of them. "More? We've got plenty."

Dylan and Angelina exchanged a look before shaking their heads. They thanked her and were just getting ready to leave when Imogene let out a squeal.

"Wait! I want to introduce you to my daughter!"

Angelina stifled a groan when she saw Christine Williams waving wildly in the distance. She was tall, blonde, beautiful, and the biggest flirt in Maple Ridge. As she strutted down the street, everyone noticed that her denim shorts just barely covered her bottom and her tank top left very little to the imagination. Neither wardrobe choice was unusual for Christy.

"Who's this?" Christy smiled up at Dylan and pointedly ignored his companion. Again, that was nothing new. Christy and Angelina had spent most of their lives trying to forget the other existed, especially after Christy's unfortunate case of pimples.

The memory never failed to make Angelina laugh.

Imogene made the introductions. "Christy is a photographer with the *Maple Ridge Gazette*. I bet the two of you have a lot in common since you're both in the news business."

Christy was her usual giggly self as she asked Dylan a hundred questions about his job in Nashville. He was polite and answered them all while Angelina took a deep breath, counted to twenty, and scanned the crowd for her mom. She wasn't hard to find, sitting under a tent and wearing her red, wide-brimmed hat. By her side was David Murray, plucking his banjo.

After five minutes of Christine's nonstop chatter, Angelina politely excused herself and walked over to the next booth. She said hello to Mrs. Evans and reached for one of her homemade candles, lifting the top and inhaling the fruity scent. Suddenly, she felt someone's hand brush the small of her back, and she smiled.

"That was quick. Christine boring you already?"

"Christine who?"

Her body went rigid.

Adam laughed. "Christine Williams? Hell, she bored me back in high school."

That wasn't how Angelina remembered it at all. Adam had always appreciated Christy's short skirts and complete lack of morals.

"Looks like your new boyfriend is enjoying her company, though."

Angelina tightly gripped the candle and turned toward her ex.

"What do you want, Adam?"

His grin was just as breathtaking as ever. Too bad she knew the evil man behind the pearly smile.

"She speaks. I was beginning to wonder."

Nervously, she glanced toward Imogene's booth to find Dylan's eyes fixated on the two of them. Christine was still chattering, but he wasn't paying her a bit of attention.

This made Angelina far happier than it should.

"By the way, don't think I didn't notice that I paid full price for that guitar. Is that any way to treat your first great love?"

"You are *not* my first great love. You were my greatest mistake."

Adam's eyes flashed with anger before he chuckled darkly.

"You look gorgeous. I'm surprised the boyfriend lets you out of his sight."

She didn't bother correcting him. Instead, Angelina paid Mrs. Evans for the candle before heading toward the next booth.

"Don't ignore me, Angelina," he said menacingly, grabbing her arm. "You know how much I hate that."

It was the same threatening tone he'd reserved for her back when they'd been dating. A sliver of fear rushed through her, leaving her breathless as she remembered his quick temper.

But she wasn't that girl anymore.

"Get your hands off me, Adam."

In an instant, Dylan was there, his eyes blazing.

"Is there a problem?"

Adam's grin was cocky. "Nope, no problem at all."

"There will be if you don't let go of her arm."

A few murmurs from the crowd prompted Adam to let her go. He cleared his throat, and the charming smile was back.

"You two enjoy the festival," he said, nodding at a few of the onlookers before walking away.

Angelina breathed a sigh of relief.

"Are you okay?" Dylan asked.

She nodded numbly.

"You're shaking," he murmured, gently prying the candle from her hand. He led her back toward the store where they sat down on the bench.

"Who is he, Angelina?"

She could hear the quiet fury in his voice, but it was different from Adam's menacing tone. Dylan was clearly pissed, but he wasn't mad at her.

"This is off the record?"

"Do you seriously think I give a shit about my article right now?"

Angelina shrugged and stared at her hands in her lap. "I can't read your mind, Dylan. I don't know what you're thinking."

He sighed and leaned back against the bench as he stared out at the festival. They grew quiet, and she took the opportunity to study his profile. He looked tortured and frustrated—two emotions she understood so well.

What she didn't understand was why he felt that way.

"His name is Adam McDonald," Angelina said. "He's my ex-boyfriend who now lives in Asheville."

"I assume it didn't end well."

"No, it didn't. He wanted to control . . . everything. My every decision. My every thought. My every move. He was manipulative and overbearing, and when I finally stood up for myself, he hit me."

Dylan eyes flashed with anger. "He *hit* you?"

"Just once, but yes."

He jumped to his feet and glanced down the street, and she knew, instinctively, who he was looking for.

"Please, don't. It was a long time ago, and I'm fine."

65

He exhaled a noisy breath and turned toward her.

"Do you really want to know what I'm thinking, Angelina?"

Do I?

"Yes, I do."

"I'm thinking that I want to beat the hell out of him for touching you."

Dylan's cell phone rang, and he excused himself to take the call. As he walked away, Angelina struggled to slow her racing heart.

"They look happy."

Celia nodded toward the street where Maddie and her boyfriend were dancing along to the bluegrass music that echoed from the stage. Nick had arrived late in the afternoon, just as he'd promised, and the two had been inseparable ever since.

"He'll be home for two weeks," Angelina said.

Celia hummed softly and sipped her lemonade while they sat on the bench outside the store. It was getting late, and Angelina knew her mom was tired from the day. She'd always loved the festival and couldn't bear to miss it, but things were winding down, and the vendors were beginning to close in anticipation of the concert.

"Dylan offered to take you home. If you're ready, I'll send him a text."

"Where is he?"

Laughing, Angelina pointed toward the booth where the football team was selling funnel cakes. "He's eaten three. I think he's in love."

"I think you're right."

She gave her daughter a pointed look, and Angelina

knew they weren't talking about funnel cakes anymore.

"I think the heat has made you a little delusional."

"Angelina, you're fighting fate. I heard about the incident over at the candle booth. Dylan is such a gentleman, coming to your rescue like that. Mrs. Evans said he was quite protective."

"Yes, and I don't understand why."

Celia offered her a weary smile. "If only you could see."

Angelina swallowed nervously. "You've . . . *seen* something?

"Yes, but I'm sure it's just another one of my delusions," she said, patting her daughter's hand. "You wouldn't be interested."

Angelina sighed heavily. *How can a mother be so infuriating?*

Celia grinned and rose to her feet. "David has offered to drive me home, so don't bother texting Dylan. It's going to be a beautiful night, and I don't want either of you missing the concert."

"David Murray?"

"Yes."

Angelina had never asked her mom about her dinner date on the night of the storm, but connecting those dots was easy now as she watched her stroll over to Mr. Murray's picnic table. She looped her arm through his, and the two of them walked toward his car. They talked and laughed, and while it was odd seeing her mom smile at a man who wasn't her father, Angelina couldn't ignore the peaceful expression on her mother's face.

In that moment, a very selfish part of Angelina was envious of her mom.

Angelina had just closed the shop and stepped back outside when she spotted Emma Riley sitting on the bench.

"Hey, Emma."

The eight-year-old smiled up at her. She looked adorable in her blonde braids and pink overalls.

"Hi, Angelina. I have a message for you."

"Oh?"

She nodded. "I get ten dollars just for asking. I get *twenty* dollars if you say yes. You really need to say yes, because I'm saving my allowance for a new bike."

Angelina laughed, and the little girl leapt up from the bench, taking her by the hand and leading her toward the crowd. People lined the street, dancing the electric slide to a cover of an old George Strait song. Angelina waved to Nick and Maddie as Emma pulled her through the dancers.

Suddenly, Emma stopped in her tracks and pointed toward one of the picnic tables.

"Will you dance with him?"

Looking up, Angelina found Dylan smiling sheepishly at her from his place on top of the table.

The girl tugged her hand. "Will you?"

Grinning, Angelina leaned down and whispered in her ear.

"Go tell him he owes you twenty bucks."

Emma giggled and raced to Dylan's side, and he promptly placed some cash in her hand. The little girl waved at him and raced toward her mother as Dylan made his way through the crowd. The melodic strains of a mandolin filled the air as he took Angelina by the hand

and pulled her close.

Naturally, the band chose that moment to play a slow song.

"Did you bribe the band, too?" Angelina asked teasingly.

"Maybe."

"Hmm. This is an expensive dance."

His arms tightened around her.

"It's worth every penny, Angelina."

They swayed to the music, and Angelina tried to ignore how good it felt to be held by someone whose touch was gentle and sweet. Throughout the song, Dylan held her a little tighter, a little closer, but it wasn't possessive or domineering. He held her hand close to his chest, and when the song transitioned into something a little more upbeat, their rhythm remained the same.

"Have I ever told you how pretty you are?"

Too dazed to answer, Angelina simply nodded. Dylan brushed his forehead against hers, and she wrapped her arms around his neck.

"I was so jealous today," he admitted.

"Why?"

"Those two guys in your shop . . . and then Adam. You just have a long string of admirers."

Angelina felt her face flush with embarrassment. "I don't have admirers."

"You do. You may not realize it—or want to admit it—but you do."

Even if she did acknowledge it, she knew it wasn't something she, or they, could really control. It was that stupid, manipulative spell.

That wasn't something Angelina could explain to him.

"There's no reason to be jealous, Dylan."

"There isn't?"

"You're the only one I've said yes to."

Their eyes remained locked as they danced, and when his gaze flickered to her mouth, she felt her heartbeat quicken.

"Why did you say yes to me?" His voice was low and seductive, and it made Angelina melt against him.

"Because Emma Riley needed the cash."

"Is that the only reason?"

Angelina's heart pounded faster when she realized the answer was no. The truth was she hadn't thought twice about dancing with him. Dylan made her feel comfortable and safe, which were two things she hadn't felt in a very long time.

"No, that's not the only reason."

Dylan stroked her cheek, his eyes scorching with need.

"I've never wanted to kiss anyone as much as I want to kiss you."

She was so torn. Was he simply spellbound and any attraction he felt nothing more than the curse? And if so, was it fair to kiss him?

Dylan lowered his head, and her head screamed, warning her that this was dangerous on so many levels.

But her heart refused to listen.

Dylan tenderly brushed his lips against hers, and for the first time in her life, she felt it—that unmistakable rush of excitement that was supposed to encompass a first kiss. It was like a jolt of energy, crackling and electric as it flowed through her veins. With a deep groan, Dylan parted his lips, kissing her a little harder. Angelina threaded her fingers in his hair, tugging him closer and wishing they were anywhere but there, and that she was just any girl kissing a cute guy in the middle of a crowded street.

But she wasn't just any girl, and it was that sobering thought that brought her back to reality.

They were both breathless when they finally pulled away.

"That was just as perfect as I imagined it would be."

Angelina lifted her eyes toward his. "You've imagined it?"

"Since the moment we met."

Too overwhelmed to respond, she bowed her head and fought to keep her tears at bay.

"Hey," he said gently, placing his finger beneath her chin and tilting her face toward his. "What's wrong?"

With his soft brown eyes staring down into hers, Angelina struggled to find the words.

Everything's wrong.

But she didn't say it.

Instead, she just smiled and let him wrap her in his arms. Dylan pulled her close to his chest as they continued to dance beneath the stars.

Seven

Dylan stared at the ceiling fan spinning above his head. It was making him a little dizzy, which was perfect, because he'd felt that way ever since that dance.

And that kiss.

Never had a kiss affected him so much. He'd dated plenty—and he'd kissed them all at least once—but this was unlike anything he'd ever experienced. She'd tasted like cinnamon, and he didn't know if that was just the natural taste of her lips or if she'd had a sweet dessert at one of the booths.

Either way, he was addicted.

His mind and body were too restless to sleep, so he quickly got dressed and decided to go for a drive.

The woman was driving him insane. He couldn't even concentrate on his article, and Steve, his editor, was breathing down his neck, asking to take a look at his notes so far. Most of it wouldn't make sense, and he knew he'd have to spend some time arranging them into some kind of coherent mess to email to the boss.

Dylan wasn't paying attention to the road until the highway suddenly transformed into gravel. Images of dueling banjos and crazy hillbillies flashed through his mind as he scanned the area, and he was just about to turn around when he came upon a wooden building with neon signs flashing in the windows.

It was a bar, tucked deep in the woods.

Dylan grinned.

Alcohol was exactly what he needed.

The bar was the biggest redneck tavern he'd ever seen in his life, but the music was loud and the beer was cheap.

Which would explain his present state of intoxication.

The bartender offered him another bottle, but Dylan declined. He needed to sober up if he had any chance of driving home tonight.

"You're that reporter from Nashville, aren't you? Doing the story on Angelina Clark and her mom."

Dylan's body shivered at the mention of her name, and he cursed under his breath. Escaping her, even in a dump like this, was impossible.

"They're good people," the bartender said.

Dylan couldn't remember his name. Mel? Max? It was an M, definitely.

"Yes, they are."

"Angelina's a sweetheart," the man continued. "That ex of hers sure treated her badly."

Dylan nodded. "He better pray I never see him again, because if I do, I'll beat the shit out of him."

The bartender grinned and pointed toward the pool tables. "Is that a promise?"

Dylan couldn't believe his eyes. Standing there, laughing and drinking with his buddies, was Adam McDonald.

They spotted each other at the same time, and Adam smirked. He said something to his friends and dropped his pool stick before heading to the bar.

"You look like you could use another," Adam said, his voice slurring a little as he waved to the bartender. He slapped Dylan on the shoulder. "Look, man, I'm going to give you a little advice. If you're waiting to get into Angelina's pants, don't bother, because you'll be waiting a long time."

Dylan's entire body bristled at the mention of her name on the bastard's lips. He wasn't so drunk that he didn't take a moment to consider the consequences of his actions.

This was a redneck bar, and it was quite possible he'd get his ass kicked.

Then he thought of Angelina's sweet face, her pretty eyes, and her cinnamon kiss.

Worth it.

The screen door gently closed as Celia made her way out onto the porch.

"Good morning, Angelina. You're up early."

"Couldn't sleep."

She patted Cash's head as he rested near the rocker. They'd already taken their morning walk to the pond. The morning was cool, a sure sign that fall was on the way.

"I made you some tea."

"Thanks," she said, taking the mug. "Do I smell peppermint?"

Celia sat down in her rocking chair. "A little. I had a feeling you might need something to relax you this morning. Call it a mother's intuition."

"Right. You knew exactly what was going to happen last night, didn't you?"

"What happened?"

Angelina sighed deeply and drank her tea.

"You know my visions aren't synchronized to a clock. I never know *when* something's going to happen."

"But you knew we'd kiss, didn't you?"

Celia's face transformed into a beautiful smile.

"Yes, but to be fair, I don't think my psychic powers were needed to make that prediction. Sparks flew from the moment you two met. Surely you aren't surprised."

The kiss itself wasn't surprising. It was her unexpected reaction to it that was throwing Angelina for a loop.

"What if it's not real?"

"What do you mean?"

"You believe in that stupid curse, right?" Angelina asked, and her mom nodded. "So, what if whatever we think we're feeling is just the spell weaving its magic on the two of us? What if it's bogus?"

Celia's face grew thoughtful. "Do you think my marriage to your father was bogus?"

"Of course not."

"Our relationship started just like this," she said, smiling at the memory. "I cast the spell when I was thirteen, just like you. Your father arrived when I was twenty-one. Granted, I didn't try to shoot him, but still, I'd like to think it was love at first sight for both of us."

Angelina groaned. "Would you please not joke about

this? I'm so confused. How can I trust how he feels? Or how I feel?"

Celia tilted her head in her daughter's direction. "That must have been some kiss."

You have no idea.

"I struggled with the same insecurities when I met your father. Did he really care for me, or was it just the spell? Could I trust his emotions? Could I trust mine?"

"Did you come to any conclusions?"

"There's something you're forgetting, Angelina, and it's the same thing I failed to remember until your grandmother pointed it out to me."

"Which is?"

"No one has cast a spell on *you*."

Angelina frowned. "What does that mean?"

"My sweet daughter, it means that whatever *you* are feeling has absolutely nothing to do with magic—not in the traditional sense, anyhow."

"I don't know what I'm feeling. Everything is so confusing, and now I'm getting all this attention from guys in town that I don't even want. All because of some ridiculous spell? I'm suddenly a magnet for men just because I turned twenty-one? How nuts is that?"

Her mom smiled. "You're a beautiful young woman. Why wouldn't they be attracted?"

"But why *now*?"

Celia laughed. "Sweetheart, I hate to break the news to you, but you've always turned heads. You're just noticing now, that's all."

The phone rang, and Celia headed inside. Cash raced behind her, leaving Angelina alone in her confusion. Closing her eyes, she traced her fingertip along her lips, recalling the heat of Dylan's kiss and how the memory of it kept her awake all night long.

No one has cast a spell on you.

"I'm not so sure about that," she whispered.

Minutes later, a laughing Celia reappeared on the porch. Angelina gave her a strange look as her mom placed a set of car keys into her hand.

"Am I going somewhere?"

"To the sheriff's department. Take your checkbook."

"Why would I need my checkbook?"

Celia was trying to stifle her laughter.

"For Dylan's bail."

"You are unbelievable, do you know that?"

Celia had warned her daughter to keep her temper in check, but the entire situation was just too ridiculous. Who gets into a drunken brawl with a complete stranger?

Dylan peered at the speedometer. "You're going to get a ticket, Angelina."

"*Now* you're worried about breaking the law?"

He groaned and closed his eyes.

"Oh, I'm sorry. Do you have a headache? Am I too *loud?*"

"I begged Celia to pick me up," he muttered under his breath. "*Begged* her."

"Why should my ailing mother have to come bail your sorry ass out of jail? What were you doing at Max's bar, anyway?"

Dylan mumbled something, but she ignored him and drove faster toward the motel. Angelina was furious. She'd spent her night tossing and turning because of his stupid kiss while he was out at some backwoods bar with God knows who, doing God knows what.

"Angelina, you're doing seventy in a forty-five."

"Stop criticizing my driving!"

But she did ease her foot off the pedal. Despite her aggravation, she didn't have a death wish.

"I'm in room fifteen," Dylan said as they turned into the parking lot.

The Maple Ridge Lodge wasn't exactly a four-star hotel. It probably didn't qualify for any stars at all, but at least it was nice and clean. Dylan invited Angelina inside, and she was surprised to find it wasn't a complete dump. The bed had been made, and there wasn't a pair of dirty underwear in sight.

He sat down on the edge of the bed and kicked off his shoes. "You look surprised."

"I am, a little."

"Not what you were expecting?"

"Not really. Most guys are pigs."

Dylan chuckled and reached for a bottle of aspirin on his nightstand. He twisted the lid off a half-empty bottle of water sitting next to his bed and downed the pills.

"Well, I'm sorry to disappoint—again."

Angelina sighed and sat down next to him. His eye was already swollen, and she noticed his hands had several small cuts along the knuckles.

"Does it hurt?"

"Nah. You should see the other guy." Suddenly, his head snapped up. "Actually, forget I said that. I don't want you to see him ever again."

She was instantly suspicious.

"You told my mom you got into a fight with someone from out of town."

He nodded and sipped his water.

"Was that a lie?"

"It wasn't a lie. You said he lives in Asheville now."

Her mouth fell open.

"*Adam*? You got into a fight with Adam McDonald?"

"Don't get pissed—"

Anger flooded her, and she jumped to her feet. "I'm already pissed! You got into a fight with Adam? Over me? What were you thinking?"

"I was thinking about you! All I ever do is think about you! Believe me, it's aggravating as hell, but it doesn't seem to be something I can control."

Too stunned to formulate a response, Angelina dropped back onto the edge of the bed. Dylan stood up and began to pace the room.

"I couldn't sleep, Angelina. All I could think about was you and that kiss, so I took a drive around town. I got lost and ended up at some hillbilly tavern on Bluebird Lane. I have no idea how much I drank, but it was too much, obviously. I was trying to sober up before I drove back to the motel, and that's when I spotted that bastard standing next to the pool table. He made some smartass comment about you, and I saw your face. When I thought about how he hurt you, I just . . . I lost it. All I could think about was kicking his ass, so that's what I did, and nobody tried to stop me. I was a complete stranger to these people, and they let me beat the crap out of him. The only reason we got arrested at all was because a deputy arrived."

Angelina wasn't too surprised that no one had rushed to Adam's defense. He'd burned a lot of bridges in Maple Ridge. His violent tendencies hadn't been limited to just her, and there were plenty of brothers and fathers still eager to get their hands on him.

Dylan sat down on the bed once again. "I waited until Adam made bail before I called your mom. I didn't want her to find us in adjoining cells. I thought seeing him might upset her, and I didn't want that. I would have called Maddie, but I don't have her number."

Angelina's heart thawed a little. He gotten into a fight and thrown into jail because of her. It was stupid and sweet and a thousand other emotions she couldn't name.

"Angelina," he said softly, turning in her direction, "I'm not rational when it comes to you. It's driving me a little nuts, to be honest. I wasn't exaggerating earlier when I said you're all I think about. I've done nothing but think about you since the moment we met. I've never been this . . . consumed by a woman before, and I have no idea how to handle it. I am so drawn to you, and I know it sounds crazy because we don't know each other at all, but I can't help how I feel. And after last night's kiss, I know you feel it, too. I know you do."

If she'd been any other woman, his speech would have sent her heart into a frantic dance. Instead, Angelina felt nothing but sadness, because she knew why he felt so consumed, and it had absolutely nothing to do with her.

He reached for her hand. "Say something, please."

They stared into each other's eyes, and she swallowed anxiously, struggling to find the words he needed to hear. Something that would explain the madness. But what could she say? *When I was thirteen years old, I wished for you?*

Anything she might say would come out wrong. Instead, she took both his hands and gently traced her fingers over the cuts along his knuckles.

"It's been a long time since I've done this, so it might

not work."

Dylan looked confused as she took a deep breath and tenderly stroked his hands. Angelina felt the tingling rush to her fingertips, and it was the heat that let her know it was working. It had been years since she'd even tried.

It only took a moment, and when Dylan finally looked down at his hands, the tiny scratches that had marred his flesh were completely healed.

"All better."

Dylan's eyes snapped to hers and then back to his hands once again. There were no cuts, no bruises, no sign that he'd been in a fight.

"How?" His eyes were wide with disbelief.

"You've probably heard that all of the women in my mother's family have certain gifts. I'm a . . . healer. And you were right. My touch heals, but it doesn't cure."

Dylan stared as his hands, as if he was trying to find some logical response to what he'd just witnessed.

It was true. It was all true.

"Which explains why you couldn't save your father," he said.

"And I won't be able to save my mom."

"But there's still hope for Celia, right?"

Tears swam in her eyes, and she nodded. Hope was all she had. There was no magical cure for cancer. No spell or enchantment that could wipe it away.

Dylan leaned closer, and she trembled as his hand cupped her face.

"You're a witch."

"A reluctant one, but yes."

Dylan chuckled and nuzzled her cheek.

"Well, that makes perfect sense because I'm pretty

sure you've performed some kind of wicked voodoo to make me fall head over heels in love with you."

Angelina knew he was only joking, but his teasing words still pierced her soul.

What if I have?

Angelina closed her eyes as he placed a soft kiss just below her ear.

Angelina was thankful when Monday morning arrived. She needed to focus on something besides her love life, and there was nothing better than Maple Ridge traffic to help a girl forget her problems.

The two-lane highway was filled with desperate passengers in their vehicles, eager to get out of town and onto the interstate. There weren't a lot of jobs in Maple Ridge, so most early morning drivers were headed to work in Gatlinburg, Pigeon Forge, or Knoxville, and *everyone* was in a hurry. Monday mornings were always the worst, and by the time she finally made it to the shop, she was frazzled and desperate for her morning caffeine. Maddie always opened the store and had Angelina's tea waiting right next to the register.

"I'm finally here!" Angelina yelled as she walked inside the shop. "Traffic was horrible and I—"

She stopped in her tracks. It was possible that her tea was right where it should have been, but she couldn't tell.

All she could see was the gigantic bouquet of yellow daisies.

A stunned Angelina walked toward the counter. Reaching forward, she gently trailed her fingers along the petals. She was suddenly reminded of those times as a little girl when she would run around the pond, plucking daisies from the grass.

"He loves me, he loves me not . . ."

Angelina's sweet memory was shattered by a high-pitched shriek coming from the back of the store.

"Aren't they gorgeous?" Maddie gushed excitedly as she hurried toward the counter. "I was such a good girl. I didn't even read the card! You have *no* idea how hard that was for me."

Angelina felt a brief stab of disappointment.

"Maddie, you should read the card. I'm sure they're for you."

She snorted. "Nick would never send me flowers. Trust me, that vase is for you. I'll even bet my paycheck they're from a certain Nashville reporter."

With trembling fingers, Angelina reached for the tiny envelope and opened the card.

Thank you for the dance.
~Dylan

"What does it say?" Maddie said, tugging roughly on her arm until Angelina had no choice but to let her see it. "Wow. That must have been some dance!"

"It was."

She squealed happily. "Tell me all about it! I want to hear every little detail and don't leave anything out."

Maddie was Angelina's best friend in the whole world, but she wasn't sure if she was ready to bare her soul just yet. Maddie had a tendency to get excited about the most inconsequential things, and confessing that she and Dylan had shared a kiss was sure to make Maddie's head explode.

"It was just one dance."

Maddie crossed her arms and tapped her foot against the tile. "Go on."

"And it was nice."

"Just nice?"

Angelina nodded.

Maddie tilted her head and studied her face. "You are the worst liar in the history of the world, and I can't believe you'd keep something like this from me. Do you know how long I've waited for someone to walk into your life and make your heart flutter? *Do you*?"

Angelina giggled. "Flutter?"

Maddie's nostrils flared, and Angelina had to bite her lip to keep from laughing.

"Angelina Clark, you are withholding information from your best friend, which can only mean one thing. That dance was *more* than nice, and it scares you to death."

The door chimed, and Angelina smiled at their first customer of the day.

"You're wrong," she whispered in Maddie's ear. "It wasn't the dance that scared me. It was the toe-curling kiss."

Maddie's hazel eyes nearly bulged out of her head, and Angelina laughed. After all, it wasn't every day her best friend was stunned speechless.

Eight

Word spread like wildfire about Dylan's fight at the tavern. The whole town was buzzing about the news reporter and how he'd defended Angelina's honor. While nobody would confirm the fight was about her, it was an easy assumption to make. They didn't know the details, but most people in Maple Ridge were aware of her history with Adam McDonald. Those same folks had watched her dance with Dylan on the night of the festival. The fact that he practically lived at the music store and had dinner at the Clark house almost every night only added fuel to the flames.

Business was slow, which wasn't unusual after the festival. Angelina had spent the morning dusting instruments and placing some online orders. She had text messaged Dylan to thank him for the flowers, but had yet to hear from him. He didn't come by at lunch, either, and she was embarrassed to admit how much that disappointed her. She was still exhausted from her sleepless weekend, and Maddie couldn't stop texting her boyfriend long enough to actually work, so when Angelina suggested they close a little early, it was hard to tell which one of them was happier.

When Angelina arrived at the house, she was surprised to find her mom walking out the door.

"You're home early," Celia said.

"Slow day at the shop. Where are you headed?"

"Did you forget? I signed up for a quilting class down at the Methodist church."

"Oh yeah. Do you need a ride?"

Celia smiled softly. "I can still drive, Angelina."

"I know you can."

She reached up and patted her daughter's face. "Dinner's in the slow cooker. I made soup and sandwiches. Something simple."

"Simple sounds great. Thanks."

Angelina waved goodbye to her mother before making her way inside. After pouring food into Cash's bowl, she collapsed against the couch and closed her eyes. She would take a nap, and when she woke up, it would be time for dinner.

And Dylan.

Her eyes snapped open.

With a groan, Angelina climbed off the couch and went to her bedroom to change. She needed a distraction—something to get her mind off him, his beautiful daisies, and the stupid spell that was making her question everything in her life.

She found her old Bon Jovi shirt and a pair of shorts

at the bottom of her drawer. After tying her sneakers and pulling her hair into a ponytail, she headed out back to her old basketball goal. Her father had built it for her when she was in elementary school. He'd even hired someone to lay a strip of asphalt and paint the lines so she could practice her free throws. Angelina wasn't tall and nowhere near good enough to play in high school, but she had always loved to come out and shoot.

Angelina grabbed the basketball out of the nearby shed and was amazed to find it wasn't completely flat. With a smile on her face, she gave it a bounce, and the sound of leather slapping the blacktop echoed through the trees. It had been a long time since she'd played, so she was definitely rusty, but this was exactly what she needed—a little exercise and a lot of distraction from the craziness of her life.

She was just running toward the goal for a layup when she heard a voice.

"You look sexy in those shorts."

Angelina gasped, and the ball flew upward, hitting the bottom of the rim.

So much for distractions.

"You scared the crap out of me, *and* you made me miss my shot."

Dylan smiled and grabbed the rebound before passing the ball back to her.

"You play?" he asked.

"*Play* is a little strong. I shoot, and sometimes, if I'm lucky, it goes in the hoop."

Angelina tossed the ball toward the net, and this time, her aim was perfect.

He nodded approvingly. "Nice shot. I played a little

in high school."

"Were you any good?"

"I was a good bench warmer. Does that count?"

She grinned and tossed him the ball. "In that case, I *suppose* you're allowed to play with me."

"That's my dream come true, you realize."

Her heart fluttered. *Fluttered.*

Maddie would be so proud.

"Just shoot the ball, Casanova."

Dylan haphazardly threw the ball, and she laughed when it completely missed the rim.

"Wow, you *are* terrible."

Dylan glared at her and tossed the ball in her direction. Bouncing it twice, Angelina lobbed it into the air, banking it off the backboard and through the hoop. She caught the rebound and passed it back. Dylan moved to the foul line and took another shot. This time, he missed the entire goal.

"This is embarrassing," he muttered, rubbing the back of his neck. "Maybe I just need some motivation."

"Like what?"

Dylan hoisted another awkward shot into the air.

"Each time I score, you have to tell me something about yourself that nobody knows. Something I can't find in my research."

Angelina smirked. "Since you've yet to hit one basket, I think my secrets are pretty safe."

"Maybe," he said, shrugging. "And if you make your shot, I'll tell you something nobody knows about me."

So tempting.

"If, by some miracle, you happen to make a bucket or two, will my secrets be in your article?"

"No, Angelina. These secrets are just for me."

The way he said her name made her spine tingle, but she shook it off.

She had a basketball game to win.

"Deal."

Dylan insisted she take the first shot, and Angelina sunk her first basket. She arched an eyebrow, waiting for him to confess one of his darkest secrets.

"I hate country music."

Angelina placed her hand over her heart and pretended to gasp for air.

"That's blasphemy, Mr. Thomas."

"I like bluegrass, though. There *is* a difference, you know."

Angelina smiled. "I know."

He took his shot, and this time, it barely missed the rim.

Angelina didn't make every basket, but she hit most, and in the process, she learned some fascinating things about Dylan Thomas. He had just turned twenty-three and had been working at the magazine for about four months. Dylan had graduated high school with a worse GPA than hers, but his SAT score was off the charts, securing his admission to Vandy. During his freshman year, he had played drums in a punk rock band. His mom—whose name was Patti—was a firm believer in creativity and free expression, but she'd grounded her then nineteen-year-old son for an entire month when he came home with a tattoo.

Dylan finally hit an easy layup and crossed his arms over his chest.

"I don't get many chances, so this better be a good one," he muttered, raising an eyebrow.

Angelina thought carefully. *What would really shock him?*

"I'm a virgin," she said.

His mouth dropped open.

Laughing, she snatched the basketball out of his hands. The ball sailed from the three-point line and circled the rim before rattling in.

Dylan sighed. "Okay, this is my deepest, darkest secret. The one you have to promise to take to your grave. Are you ready?"

She nodded eagerly.

"My favorite movie is *The Little Mermaid*."

Angelina bowed her head in defeat and tossed the ball into the air. There was no way she could top that one. The basketball bounced in the distance, and a brief moment of silence hung between them until she erupted into a fit of giggles.

"I'm . . . sorry." Angelina tried to catch her breath as the chuckles subsided. Dylan disappeared for a second and returned with the basketball under his arm.

"You think that's funny?"

"I think that's hilarious."

Dylan grinned and took a step closer. He was breathless and sweaty, and his bangs hung loosely across his forehead. Without thinking twice, Angelina stepped forward, closing the distance between them. He glanced down at her lips, and Angelina's breath hitched in her throat.

"If I make this next shot, you have to let me kiss you," he said. "If I hit it from the three-point line, you have to let me kiss you *twice*."

Angelina didn't like the odds. She really wanted him to kiss her, but he'd only made two shots the entire game and both had been within four feet of the goal.

She needed a counter offer.

"I think you should let me shoot them for you."

Dylan grinned. "No way. I want to earn my kisses—fair and square."

Angelina sighed resignedly and watched as he placed his feet at the line. It was ridiculous, she thought, relying on some stupid three-point shot when, clearly, they both wanted this kiss to happen. The probability of him making this basket was about as good as Angelina winning the lottery.

Dylan eyed the goal, gave the ball two forceful bounces, and tossed it into the air. For the first time, his follow-through was perfect, and his jump wasn't awkward at all. It was strong, graceful, and flawless.

And it was nothing but net.

All she could do was stare at the goal with her mouth wide open as the ball rolled away.

"By the way, did I mention I set a state record for the most three-pointers scored in a single high school game?"

Bench warmer, my ass.

"Dylan Thomas, did you just hustle me?"

Grinning, he shrugged and moved closer. Angelina shivered when he touched her cheek.

"Did you really like the daisies?" he asked softly.

"I loved them."

He trailed his finger along her bottom lip.

Boldly, Angelina reached for the back of his neck and tugged him closer, pulling his lips to hers. Dylan groaned and lifted her into his arms. She wrapped her legs around his waist, holding on tightly as he carried her away from the court. Their mouths remained connected, even when she felt her back being pressed against something solid and cold.

It had to be the metal shed. The house was too far away.

Angelina's body tingled, desperate to have his hands and lips on every single part of her. The mere thought made her moan, which only encouraged him to kiss her harder.

She had never felt so desired.

Dylan buried his face against her neck while she clung to him. His strong arms held her against his chest, murmuring her name against her skin as he trailed his lips along her throat.

Dylan lifted his head, and his scorching gaze met hers. Tenderly, he kissed the tip of her nose and along her cheek, until his lips found hers once more. This kiss was slower and sweeter, and they tasted and teased as their breathing returned to normal.

Dylan kissed her one last time before lowering her to the ground. Angelina's legs nearly buckled, and his smile was smug as she grabbed on to his shoulders for support.

"Proud of yourself?"

Dylan grinned. "Best basketball game ever."

"I couldn't agree more," she replied, smiling up at him. "I learned the most fascinating things about you.

"Oh yeah? What was your favorite?"

Angelina began to sing the lyrics of Ariel's song from *The Little Mermaid*, and Dylan's eyes flashed with a mixture of laughter and excitement.

His voice was soft and low. "As if you aren't sexy enough in your Bon Jovi shirt and your tiny shorts, now you're singing to me? It's no wonder I can't control myself.

How could I possibly resist you?"

She sighed softly when he kissed her forehead. His words made her heart ache, because she knew resisting was hopeless. His feelings were overwhelming and uncontrollable because that's how the spell was intended.

It was cruel and unfair, to both of them.

And Angelina was powerless to stop it.

"Good morning, Angelina," Maddie sang as she breezed into the shop. "Isn't it a beautiful morning? The birds are singing, the sun is shining . . ."

Maddie had always been one of those irritating early birds who genuinely loved waking up at the crack of dawn, so this level of enthusiasm didn't alarm Angelina. What did concern her was the dreamy look on her best friend's face.

"I thought you were taking the day off?"

"I am, but I have *so* much to tell you!"

Angelina bit back a jealous groan. "Is this about sex? Because if so, you can spare me the details."

"Look!" Maddie thrust her left hand in Angelina's face, and there, on her ring finger, was a sparkling diamond.

Angelina gasped. "You're engaged?"

"I'm engaged!"

With a smile as bright as the sun, Maddie told her all about Nick's sweet proposal and their plans for a quickie wedding.

"When we were kids, you always said you wanted a fancy ceremony. We can't possibly get everything planned in just a month."

"A big wedding doesn't seem so important anymore. Life is just too short. You know that better than anyone."

Maddie smiled wistfully and sighed. "I just want to be his wife. I want us to be in the same house, in the same town, for as long as we both shall live."

"Oh, Maddie, I'm so happy for you!"

Maddie was bouncing. "You'll be my maid of honor?"

"Of course!"

They hugged, and when Maddie pulled away, Angelina couldn't help but notice the sudden frown on her friend's face.

"What's wrong?"

"There's something else I have to tell you," Maddie said quietly. "Nick's been offered a job with a trucking company in Atlanta. He'd still be on the road, just not as much, and it will be local runs. It's a fantastic opportunity for him, with steady pay and stable hours."

Angelina's heart clenched.

"You're moving away?"

Maddie nodded. "That's another reason we're getting married so soon. I'm already calling chapels in Gatlinburg, trying to get us booked. We won't even have time for a honeymoon before he starts his new job."

It wasn't as if Angelina had expected them to grow old and gray together in Maple Ridge. Maddie was a free spirit and had always dreamed of traveling the world. Atlanta wasn't exactly a tropical paradise, but it was a start. Nick was a good guy, and she deserved to be happy. Still, Maddie was leaving, and for a selfish moment, Angelina wondered how she'd ever live without her best friend. They'd been together since they were kids, and Maddie had stood by her side during the whole mess with Adam and through the agony of her dad's illness and his death.

Maddie had been Angelina's anchor through so many storms, and now she was moving away.

Maddie watched her friend closely, her eyes wide and hopeful as she gauged Angelina's reaction.

This is not the time to be selfish, Angelina told herself, so she swallowed the lump in her throat and blinked back her tears.

"So, when are we looking at dresses?"

Maddie beamed.

Nine

When Angelina arrived home, she was surprised to find her mom lying on the couch. A protective Cash was standing guard by her side. Angelina kneeled next to the chair. "Mom? Are you feeling okay?"

Celia sighed and opened her eyes. "Just a little nauseated and weak today. I'm sorry I haven't started dinner—"

"Don't apologize," Angelina said softly, adjusting the damp washcloth against her mom's forehead. This was part of the process, and they both understood that. Good days. Bad days. Times when she felt like she could run a marathon and others when she couldn't drag herself out of bed. Angelina knew they had been lucky with the vomiting and fatigue so far, but it still broke her heart to see her mom so frail and exhausted.

Celia didn't like to take the anti-nausea pills Dr. Campbell had prescribed. She preferred to use peppermint extract or ginger root to combat the nausea that almost always accompanied her chemo treatments. That evening, however, when Angelina offered to get the medication, her mom didn't put up a fight. Fighting back her tears, Angelina helped her mom to her bedroom and stayed by her side until Celia drifted off to sleep.

Dylan finally organized his notes and emailed them to Steve, his editor at the magazine. Luckily, Steve was impressed with his thorough investigation, but Dylan grew nervous when the word *deadline* began creeping into the phone conversation. They didn't settle on a date, which was fine for the moment, but Dylan knew the clock had officially started to tick.

Steve would give him a deadline.

Soon.

To be honest, Dylan had plenty of information to write his story. He'd talked to dozens of people and had seen and heard enough to know that there were, indeed, witches in Maple Ridge. He could probably write an entire book about Abigail Rose, but his magazine wanted a story about Appalachian folklore and present-day witchcraft in the hills. While he had more than enough details to write a lengthy article about Angelina and her mother, he couldn't deny that his heart just wasn't in it.

Still, he continued his research. Shirley, the librarian, had given him his own table in the nonfiction section where the folklore books and journals had taken up permanent residence. He was currently studying Appalachian potions and enchantments—and most of it was pretty ridiculous—but when the librarian mentioned a love spell, Dylan's inquisitive ears perked up.

"Love spell?"

"Originally conjured by Abigail Rose," Shirley said. Dylan grinned at the note of reverence in the elderly woman's voice. He heard it all the time. To the people of Maple Ridge, Abigail was still considered a saint.

"Nathaniel Rose was a boozing womanizer who abused his wife. Remember what I said about his death?"

Dylan checked his notes on his laptop. "Liver failure, right?"

The librarian nodded. "Abigail claimed he'd accidentally eaten poisonous mushrooms while out hunting, but many believed she'd just grown tired of the nightly beatings and her husband's philandering ways. A distant cousin claimed that Abigail had crumbled a little mushroom into her husband's stew. Of course, no one knows for certain, but Nathaniel died three days later."

Interesting.

"So what does that have to do with a love spell?"

Before she could answer, a group of school-aged kids rushed into the library. Shirley headed to the checkout counter while Dylan flipped through the book of spells, searching for any information about Abigail's love charm.

The noise in the library quickly became deafening, so Dylan gave up. With a tired sigh, he closed his laptop and waved to the librarian before heading to his vehicle.

Dylan planned to ask Angelina about her grandmother's supposed love spell, but when he arrived at the house and found Angelina crying on couch, his research was immediately forgotten.

"Hey," he said, kneeling in front of her. "What's wrong?"

"Just a bad day." Angelina sniffled quietly, and his

heart broke when he saw her red-rimmed eyes.

Dylan sat down on the couch and pulled her into his lap. Angelina went eagerly, wrapping her arms around his neck while he held her close. Quiet sobs wracked her body as she buried her face against his neck. He had no idea what was wrong, and he didn't ask. He just stroked her back, soothing and soft, and after a while, her tears finally calmed.

Angelina rested her head against his chest as he nuzzled her hair.

"Better?" Dylan murmured.

She nodded.

"Are you hungry? I could make something. I'll try very hard not to burn down the house."

Angelina's soft giggle was music to his ears.

"Actually, I'd like to check on my mom, but . . . after that, there's a place I would like to go," she said, smiling at him through her tears. "Will you come with me?"

Dylan nodded. She had no way of knowing, but he would follow her anywhere.

"That's the Big Dipper," Dylan said softly, pointing toward the northern sky.

Angelina knew he was trying to distract her with his constellation talk, but all she could really concentrate on was how nice it felt to be nestled against his side. They were lying on a blanket in the grass while Cash splashed happily in the pond. The mosquitoes were being merciful, letting them have the peaceful moment without too much interference. Their hands were laced together and their heads were close as they gazed at the stars.

Angelina took a deep breath.

"Mom was so sick today. I'd forgotten how lucky we'd been with the chemo. When I came home, she was just lying on the couch, too queasy to even lift her head. It was heartbreaking seeing her that way. I'd forgotten . . ."

Her voice trailed off, and Dylan rose on his elbow, gazing down at her. Dipping his head, he gently kissed her forehead, and she sighed.

"I never forget that she's sick," Angelina continued, "but sometimes, especially on her good days, it's easy to pretend everything is normal. But nothing's normal. Nothing will ever be normal."

"She could still beat this."

"I know, but there will still be yearly tests, and my heart will die a little each and every time we step into that oncologist's office. Our *normal* is gone forever, no matter what."

Angelina felt so selfish, but between Maddie's news and her mother's illness, she needed to talk to someone.

"Thank you for listening."

Dylan smiled and gently squeezed her hand. "I'll always listen."

Angelina sighed and focused her attention on the sky once more.

"I bet the stars aren't this pretty in Nashville."

Dylan chuckled. "You'd win that bet. You can barely see them in the city."

"To me, they're just little specks of light in the sky. I take them for granted."

Dylan gazed down at her. Although he knew she was worried about her mom, he couldn't help but think something else was bothering her. His suspicions were confirmed when Angelina told him about Maddie's move to Atlanta.

"They're getting married before they go," Angelina explained. "Not only am I losing my business partner, but I'm losing my best friend. I know it sounds selfish—and I'd never say that to her—but it's just another reminder that I don't value people while I have them in my life. I wait until they're leaving. Or worse—I wait until they're *gone*."

He hated hearing the bitterness in her voice. "You're not being selfish. Your mom is sick and your best friend is moving away. You have every right to vent. And I know you'll miss Maddie, but you're forgetting one important thing."

"Which is?"

"It's just Georgia. You can always visit."

Angelina nodded. "One hundred ninety-six miles."

"You already have a route mapped out, don't you?"

"Yep."

"See? That isn't far at all. It's actually farther to Nashville."

Angelina's face flickered with sadness.

"Everybody leaves."

Dylan let go of her hand and placed his palm on her cheek. Tilting her face toward his, he smiled down at her. "So we should appreciate them while they're here."

Sliding her hand along the back of his neck, Angelina pulled his lips to hers. Dylan moaned quietly, gliding his hand up her thigh and along her stomach as they kissed.

"Angelina," he murmured, trailing his lips down her neck.

Their touches were intense, but they weren't frantic. Dylan kissed her slowly and sweetly, and while it was maddening on so many levels, he knew it was what she needed.

Angelina needed him to be gentle. She needed him to be tender.

When he opened his eyes, he found her piercing blues staring up at him. Dylan trailed his fingertip along her eyebrow and down her nose before pausing at her lips. Angelina puckered and placed a soft kiss against his finger.

"I know it's a little late now, but I have to ask. Is there a girlfriend waiting for you back in Nashville?"

"No, but if there were, I'd dump her immediately."

"Well, that seems kind of rude," she teased.

Their laughter faded as Dylan pulled her hand close to his chest, letting it rest against his pounding heart.

"Do you feel that, Angelina? My heart has never beaten so fast, and it only does that when I'm with you."

Dylan kissed her once more before rolling onto his back. He pulled her into his arms, and Angelina rested her head against his chest, closing her eyes as she listened to his racing heart.

He didn't know it, but hers was hammering just as fast.

Maybe faster.

Celia was feeling much better the next morning. She even managed to eat some scrambled eggs, much to Angelina's delight. Because Celia felt guilty for starving him the night before, Dylan had been invited to breakfast.

This also made Angelina happy, and she couldn't believe the difference in her outlook. She felt a little lighter, a little hopeful. And it was all because of the man at her side, with his arm resting casually on the back of her chair. They would sneak little glances at each other, and when Celia would turn toward the stove, Dylan would nuzzle Angelina's hair. It was becoming increasingly difficult for the two of them to keep their hands to themselves.

If Celia noticed, she didn't mention it. Instead, her mom smiled and sipped her peppermint tea while Angelina and Dylan held hands beneath the table.

"Dylan, how's your article coming along?" Celia asked.

"I actually wanted to talk to you about something I read, if you're feeling up to it. Would you mind?"

"Not at all."

Dylan pushed his empty plate aside. "Well, I was doing research at the library yesterday, and Shirley told me about Abigail Rose and some kind of love spell."

Angelina's fork froze mid-air.

"According to the book," Dylan continued, "Abigail was so heartbroken over the death of her husband that she and her sisters conjured some kind of love charm, hoping their daughters would never have to endure the pain of a lost love."

Close.

Mother and daughter exchanged a look.

"I know there was some controversy surrounding her husband's sudden death," Dylan said, oblivious to the sudden tension in the air, "but, if the stories are true, Nathaniel Rose wasn't Husband of the Year, so I can't see her being too choked up that he was gone."

Angelina couldn't believe all the evidence he'd found at their little local library. Who knew the tiny place and the old woman behind the checkout counter were both such endless wells of useful information?

Dylan looked between the two of them.

"So . . . I guess what I'm asking is if any of this is true? Did Abigail Rose murder her husband? And did she and her sisters conjure some kind of love spell?"

Celia cleared her throat and carefully chose her words.

"Obviously, we can't confirm or deny if Abigail killed her husband. Nobody can. And as far as a love spell, our ancestors were famous for casting many hexes and enchantments."

Dylan looked to Angelina. "Can you do that? Cast spells, I mean?"

"I *can*. I just choose not to."

"But you have?"

Angelina nodded slowly.

"We all have," Celia told him. "When I was nine, I accidentally cast a spell on a boy who'd pulled my hair on the school playground. He had warts for a month."

Everyone laughed, and Angelina breathed a sigh of relief as her mom effectively distracted the clever reporter from any discussion about the love charm.

Ten

The rest of the week passed slowly, and visitors to the shop were few and far between. Online orders were keeping the store afloat, and Angelina was thankful she had taken the time to form strong relationships with her national vendors and musicians.

While the slump in local sales left Angelina with too much time on her hands, it seemed Dylan was busier than ever. He was constantly interviewing people and doing research for the article, and whenever she would ask how it was coming along, he'd admit it was still a work in progress and then quickly change the subject. Angelina had a feeling he was dragging his feet, and when she mentioned this to her mother, Celia would smile her irritating, omniscient smile.

Angelina was just getting ready to close another dismal day at the shop when the door chimed. Christine Williams walked in, wearing a pink halter-top and her mandatory skimpy denim shorts. She sashayed over to the counter, and Angelina resisted the urge to roll her eyes. *Who is she trying to impress?*

"Hello, Angelina."

"Hey, Christy. What can I do for you?"

She leaned her elbows against the glass counter and smacked her gum. "I was actually looking for Dylan. Has he been around today?"

Angelina clasped her hands tightly around the edge of the counter.

"No, I haven't seen him."

She frowned. "Well, do you have his number? I'd love to get in touch with him."

It was irrational, the spike of jealousy that shot through her veins.

"I wouldn't feel comfortable giving out his number without his permission," Angelina replied. "If I see him, I'll let him know you're looking for him."

Christy tilted her head to the side.

"Everyone in town thinks you're dating. Is that true?"

What could she say? *We haven't actually gone out on a date. He's just the victim of the cruelest love spell in the history of magic?*

"No, we aren't dating." It was the truth, after all.

Christy's face brightened. "Really? So, you wouldn't mind if I asked him out?"

Angelina was sure she felt the blood drain from her face. The thought of Christy anywhere near Dylan filled her with rage, but what could she do? They had made no promises to each other.

"No, Christine," Angelina murmured, dying a little inside. "I wouldn't mind at all."

Dylan was regretting his visit to the offices of the *Maple Ridge Gazette* for two very distinct reasons.

The archival collection was in shambles, and Christine Williams wouldn't leave him the hell alone.

He probably could have handled the first issue if there had been any rhyme or reason to their filing system. It wouldn't have been the first time he had to wade through mounds of newspapers to find one nugget of information that might prove useful for a story, but finding anything worthwhile in this mess would take him weeks, and he just wasn't that desperate for facts.

But now, he was searching through slides on the microfiche machine, and Christy was getting on his nerves. She was sitting far too close, and she smelled far too much like cotton candy.

Dylan hated cotton candy.

He was a man, and it wasn't as if he couldn't appreciate her tiny shorts and long legs, but he just wasn't interested. She'd been overly helpful, and he'd been patiently polite, but his tolerance was about to snap. He was glad these were his last set of slides, although he was disappointed that he had wasted his time. There wasn't a thing in the articles he didn't already know.

"See anything you like?" Christy asked, brushing her arm against his shoulder.

He wasn't an idiot. He knew her question was dripping with innuendo.

"Actually, not a thing here interests me."

"You're right. This place is boring," she replied, clearly not getting the hint. "We should have dinner tonight."

Dylan had to hand it to her. She sure was persistent.

"Sorry, Christy, but I'm busy tonight. I have a lot of research to do."

"You have to eat."

"I'm having dinner with Angelina and Celia, like I do most nights."

Christy's eyes danced with mischief. "I had a nice chat with Angelina today."

Dylan felt an inexplicable pain in his chest at the mention of her name. He hadn't spoken to her since last night. It was ridiculous that he missed her so much.

"It's funny," Christy continued. "The whole town thinks the two of you are together, but Angelina certainly squashed that rumor today."

He stilled. "What do you mean?"

"She told me the two of you aren't dating. She even said she wouldn't mind at all if the two of *us* had dinner tonight."

His hands balled into fists at his side.

"Well, like I said. I'm busy, Christine."

He began to gather his belongings, desperate to be out of this room and away from the sickening smell of her perfume.

"What about coffee tomorrow morning?"

"Fine. Coffee. Whatever."

Once he was out in the parking lot—and away from Christy's nauseating scent—he still felt as if he'd been punched in the gut. It was in that moment Dylan realized two things.

He was in love with Angelina Clark.

And she had absolutely no idea.

"Dylan isn't coming for dinner tonight," Celia announced

as Angelina made her way into the kitchen. Her mom was standing next to the stove, stirring a gigantic pot of chili. "He didn't sound too happy on the phone. Did you two have another argument?"

Angelina peeked over her mom's shoulder. "That smells good. And no, I haven't talked to him since last night. He's been spending a lot of time at the library doing research for his article. That thing could be a full-length novel by the time he gets it finished."

Celia laughed. "I'm glad to hear the two of you are getting along. Things are progressing nicely?"

This was her mother's not-so-subtle way of asking if they'd kissed again.

"Things are . . . confusing."

"Only because you're making them so."

Angelina finished setting the table. It felt strange, needing just two glasses and bowls. Dylan rarely missed the chance for a home-cooked meal.

Maybe he's having dinner with Christine tonight.

Her stomach lurched.

"Angelina, are you okay? You don't look well."

She took a deep breath and sat down at the table. "I'm fine."

Celia placed her palm against her daughter's forehead. "Are you sure? You look a little pale."

"You don't need to call a doctor," Angelina said, smiling up at her mother. "Let's eat before it gets cold."

Angelina scooped chili into their bowls while her mom grabbed the milk from the fridge.

"Speaking of doctors, my oncologist called today. I have an appointment Thursday afternoon."

Angelina had been expecting this. It was time to see if

the chemo had done its job.

"Okay. I'll make sure Maddie's free to watch the shop."

They swiftly changed the subject, and Angelina finally had the chance to tell her mom about Maddie's engagement and her move to Atlanta.

"She's absolutely right," Celia said when Angelina mentioned her friend's plans for a quickie wedding. "Life is too short to waste it making plans for a big ceremony. Why spend months making preparations for your life together when you could be *living* it?"

This heavy conversation—not to mention her anxiety about Dylan's whereabouts—had ruined Angelina's appetite. Her mom, unfortunately, was keeping a watchful eye on the bowl, so Angelina forced herself to eat every bite.

As the night progressed, Angelina had a sinking feeling in the pit of her stomach. Dylan hadn't called. He hadn't even sent a text, and that was unusual. Either he had gotten lost in his research, or he was with a girl who was flirty, sexy, and far more experienced than Angelina could ever hope to be.

I never should have told him I'm a virgin.

Angelina wasn't innocent by any stretch of the imagination, but technically, she was still pure as the driven snow. Adam had tried his best to convince her otherwise, but she had been adamant about waiting until she turned twenty-one, just in case the spell proved to be legit. Of course, that was before her father's illness—back when she had been young and foolish and waiting for her soul mate to arrive. If their heated kisses on the ball court and their make-out session by the pond were any indication, Dylan was a passionate and loving man.

And Angelina had offered him on a silver platter to the biggest flirt in town.

It was nearly dawn by the time she drifted off to sleep. Her mind was still restless, conjuring nightmares filled with Christine's irritating laugh and Dylan's sweet smile.

"*What* did you do?"

"I've had exactly one hour of sleep. I'm afraid you're going to have to be a little more specific," Angelina muttered as she dusted the shelves.

Maddie crossed her arms. "I just saw Dylan at the coffee shop. He had two drinks in his hand, so I assumed one was for you. When I told him you preferred tea, he mumbled something and headed straight toward a back booth. Do you know who was sitting at the table with him?"

Angelina shrugged casually.

"What did you *do*, Angelina?"

She sighed. "Christy asked if Dylan and I were dating."

"And what did you say?"

"I said we aren't, which is true, and he obviously agrees."

"I wouldn't bet on it. The man looked as if he'd rather be getting a root canal than having coffee with her."

Angelina couldn't deny she was impressed. Christy sure moved fast. They'd probably had dinner, too. Maybe Dylan had even spent the night.

"You look nauseous," Maddie mumbled.

At her friend's insistence, Angelina headed home to

take a nap. Her mom was spending the day in town with Mr. Murray, so she had the house all to herself. She decided to take a warm bath, hoping the water would soothe her tired muscles and relax her mind.

It didn't.

Feeling more awake after the bath, she decided to take her dog for a walk. Cash led her straight to the pond, and it was only when her eyes focused on the water did she understand why.

Of course he was there, sitting on the grass.

Dylan turned his head when he heard Cash's enthusiastic bark. Her dog deserted her, rushing toward Dylan and pouncing excitedly on his friend's back. By the time Angelina arrived at the pond, Cash was already splashing in the water.

"Hey," she said softly, sitting down next to him.

"Hey."

"What are you doing?"

Dylan tossed a rock across the water, causing ripples to form along the surface. "I have no idea what I'm doing, and I don't know why I'm here."

"It's okay that you're here. You're welcome, anytime."

"That's not what I meant." With a sigh, he turned toward her. "You need to know I've had zero sleep, so my verbal filter is going to be nonexistent today."

"I was up all night, too."

"Thinking about us?"

Angelina nodded.

Dylan took a deep breath. "Maybe I'm going insane. It wouldn't surprise me. I've never felt like this. My attraction to you is so confusing, and I have no idea what you're thinking. I don't know how you feel, and maybe you don't feel anything, but you kiss me like you feel something, and I—"

"I feel something."

"You do?"

"Yes."

"Then why?"

Angelina swallowed nervously. "Why what?"

"Why did you tell Christy Williams that you didn't mind if she asked me out?"

The question hung in the air while she struggled to find the words.

"You don't belong to me, Dylan."

He laughed quietly and looked down, lacing his fingers with hers.

"You're wrong. You have no idea how much I belong to you."

Angelina closed her eyes, letting the warmth of his words wash over her.

"Everything about you fascinates me, Angelina. The way your hand fits in mine. Your soft giggle when something is truly funny. Your fingers when you play your guitar. The love you have for your dog. The way you worry about your mother, even though you try to hide it. Your lips. They taste like cinnamon. Did you know that?"

A stunned Angelina shook her head.

"The list is endless, and I know it makes me sound deranged, but that's how I feel." Dylan reached over, smoothing a strand of hair away from her face. "Yesterday, something became very clear to me."

"What was that?"

"You have absolutely no idea of the hold you have on

my heart."

It was the sweetest thing anyone had ever said to her.

"You weren't tempted by Christy? Not even a little?"

He looked confused. "Why would I be tempted by her?"

"Because she's pretty."

"She's not you."

"She's—"

"Angelina, stop." He gently placed his hands on each side of her face, forcing her to look into his eyes. "I don't care what she is. She's not *you*."

Dylan kissed her tenderly, and in that moment, her heart ached with the realization that she couldn't deny it any longer.

She was spellbound.

And so was he.

With that acceptance came a crushing wave of sadness, because she wanted, so much, for this to be real. Dylan's emotions were ruled by the spell, and while she loved the taste of his lips and the warmth of his body as he lowered her down onto the grass, it was impossible to let herself be swept away by the magic of it all.

Because that's all it was.

Magic.

She gazed up at him, caressing his cheek and loving the feel of his stubble against her palm.

"Angelina, why are you fighting this?"

"Because it's not real."

"It feels very real to me."

"I know."

Even she could hear the sadness in her voice, and it was enough to make him roll over onto his back.

Breathing harshly, he covered his eyes with his arm.

"Angelina, you're killing me."

She sat up, hugging her knees close to her chest. "I know, and I'm sorry. I'm sorry about everything. I'm sorry about Christine, and I'm sorry you're feeling the way you feel, and I'm sorry it's not real."

Sighing heavily, Dylan sat up beside her. Goosebumps erupted on her skin as he softly trailed his fingers across her arm.

"Why do you keep saying that?"

She had to make him understand, and the only way to do that was to tell him the truth.

"Do you remember what you found in your research? About Abigail and the love charm?"

He nodded.

"When I was growing up, I couldn't wait until I turned thirteen, because that's the age when the daughter is allowed to cast her own spell. She wishes for happiness, beauty, gifts, and intelligence. And she wishes for her soul mate—a man who will be kind and loving and devoted, until death do them part. Then the daughter blows out the candle, and she waits."

She knew it sounded completely ridiculous.

Dylan blinked rapidly. "She *waits*?"

"Yes."

"How long does she wait?"

"Until she turns twenty-one. I know it sounds crazy, but as a little girl, it was the ultimate fairy tale, and I believed it with my whole heart. Then I grew up, and my supposedly gifted hands weren't magical enough to heal my father. The day they laid him in the ground was the day I buried my faith in magic."

Her shaking voice trailed off as she waited for Dylan to connect the dots. It didn't take him long.

"The day I arrived in Maple Ridge was your twenty-first birthday."

"Yes."

"You hated me on sight."

"*Hate's* a little strong . . ."

"You pointed a gun at me!"

"It wasn't loaded!"

Dylan smirked, and they both laughed. He moved closer, sliding his hand along the nape of her neck. His touch was soft and soothing, and she felt her body finally begin to relax.

"I want to know more about this spell," Dylan murmured.

"What do you want to know?"

"Well, for starters, how does it affect the man?"

Angelina sighed. "Well, once they meet, the man is completely infatuated. The attraction is immediate, and if my parents are any indication, it's eternal. The guy is consumed with thoughts of her—to the point of obsession. In his eyes, she's perfect, and no one else comes close to comparing to her . . . or so I'm told."

Dylan couldn't deny he was grateful to have the insanity explained. He wasn't losing his mind after all. There was a logical explanation, even if the logic was shrouded in the supernatural.

"That's . . . amazingly accurate."

A single tear streamed down her cheek, and he reached over, tenderly wiping it away with his fingers.

"You think my feelings for you aren't real because of some spell you conjured when you were thirteen?"

Angelina nodded.

"What I feel for you is real, Angelina. Spell or no spell."

"You can't be sure of that."

He gently tilted her face toward his.

"I'm crazy about you. I've never been more certain of anything in my entire life."

He kissed her then, and for a few glorious moments, Angelina allowed herself to believe him. She poured her heart and soul into their kiss, fearful he would come to his senses whenever he pulled away.

But he didn't.

Instead, he leaned back against the grass, pulling her close. Angelina laid her head against his chest, sighing contently as he trailed his fingers through her hair.

"It's real, Angelina," he murmured, holding her tight.

A lullaby, filled with the sounds of rippling water and his gentle heartbeat, flooded her senses and calmed her mind, and she closed her eyes.

Eleven

Dylan opened his eyes to find Angelina still sleeping peacefully in his arms. Sighing contently, he buried his nose in her hair, breathing her in.

There wasn't a doubt in his mind that he was spellbound.

Whether he believed in magic was irrelevant. From the moment they met, he had been irrationally attracted to her. Dylan didn't believe his feelings were being manipulated by some charm she had chanted when she was a little girl, but he couldn't deny the power of the force that had brought them together.

Dylan trailed his fingers against her spine as he contemplated his next move. First, he needed to have a conversation with his editor, because this story was dead in the water. There was no way he could write a feature about Angelina and her family. He wouldn't expose them to that kind of publicity. He loved them too much, and he refused to make a quick buck by sharing their secrets with the world.

Steve could fire him for all he cared.

Unfortunately, that conversation would require a trip to Nashville, which probably wasn't a bad thing. He could spend some time with his mom, deal with his boss, and try to wrap his head around everything Angelina had told him.

His arms tightened around her. The thought of being without her, even for a few days, was hard to imagine.

But it had to be done.

Angelina snuggled deeper into his arms, and he smiled.

"How long did we sleep?" she asked groggily.

"Just a few hours."

Dylan kissed the top of her head. This was a level of contentment he had never dreamed existed, but it did. It was right here in his arms, and he didn't care if it took the rest of his life to prove to Angelina that his feelings for her were the real thing.

"Angelina?"

"Hmm?"

"I've been thinking about everything you said, and I think . . . I think I need to go home for a couple of days. See my mom. Meet with my editor. Maybe some distance will help me make sense of all this."

"But you'll come back, right?"

She sounded so unsure, and it killed him.

"Sweetheart, look at me," he whispered. With her head still resting against his chest, she tilted her face toward his. "I'm coming back, and when I do, I'll be a man on a mission to prove you're all I want—spell or no spell."

Two days passed, and Angelina thought she was handling

things pretty well. She had only cried once. Twice. Maybe three times.

Honestly? She'd lost count.

Dylan called every night, telling her about his day with his mom or his conversations with his editor. He ended every phone call by saying how much he missed her, and she had been greeted each morning with a text message saying the same thing.

Anxiety had taken up permanent residence inside her chest. Would he come back? Angelina's greatest fear was that he would get home and decide he wanted no part of her ancestors' magical matchmaking. An ache filled her, and it was unlike anything she'd ever felt before. If this was love, she had no idea how her mother had survived the death of her husband. Angelina, at least, could hold on to the hope that Dylan would come back.

It only cemented Angelina's belief that Celia Clark was the strongest woman she had ever known.

Dr. Campbell's building was stark white and cold, but at least they had been allowed to wait in his comfortable office instead of the examining room.

"This is nice," Celia said, sliding her hands along the expensive chair.

"Oh yeah. You should always be sitting in a cozy leather chair as you wait to hear if your cancer has stabilized."

"Angelina . . ."

She shrugged. Her sadness and anxiety were making her a little sarcastic.

"When is Dylan coming home?"

She knows me so well.

"He thinks sometime next week," Angelina replied.

"He has some loose ends to tie up with his boss, whatever that means."

Looking up, Angelina found her mother smiling at her. Her blue eyes were peaceful and calm. Angelina couldn't believe it. They were sitting in the doctor's office, awaiting vital test results, and cancer was the very last thing on her mom's mind. Celia was thinking of her daughter, always.

"You miss him."

"Mom, it's not important. Not today."

"Of course it's important. You aren't sleeping. You're barely eating."

How does she know?

"It's . . . hard to explain."

"You don't have to explain anything to me," her mom said with a smile. "It's very overwhelming, isn't it?"

Angelina nodded. "Why do I miss him so much?"

"Because you love him."

The simple words settled into her heart and soul.

I love him.

"You make it sound so easy. You made it *look* easy."

"Nothing in life is easy, Angelina."

Angelina glanced around at the cold and sterile office. "Like cancer."

Celia sighed deeply. "The disease itself isn't what's so tough. Not for me. What's hardest for me is that my daughter has had to watch both her parents endure it. It will always be the greatest heartache of my life, knowing I've caused you pain."

Angelina grabbed her mother's hand. "*You* are not causing me pain, and *we* are going to beat this."

Celia smiled just as the door opened. Dr. Campbell

walked inside, greeting both of them with firm handshakes before sitting down behind his desk. He opened the file in his hands and scanned the page before looking up at the two of them. Typically, Dr. Campbell wore a poker face, especially when dispensing bad news, but he'd been her father's oncologist and now he was her mother's. The man had practically become a member of the family over the past three years, and Angelina could tell by the expression on his face the news wasn't good.

She listened, stunned and speechless, as he explained that he'd hoped the single mastectomy, along with the chemo treatments, would have been enough. But cancer cells had now been found in her mother's second breast, and a complete mastectomy would have to be performed. Another round of chemo would be necessary, and a more aggressive drug—with a long list of side effects that sounded worse than the cancer itself.

Angelina was enraged. "So it was all for nothing? The treatments she's had to undergo for weeks? They were all for nothing?"

Her mom's voice was soft and reassuring. "We knew a complete mastectomy was possible, Angelina."

"Possible is *not* definite."

Angelina didn't understand. Wasn't her mom pissed? Wasn't she sick of the needles and the prodding and the nausea?

The doctor gave Angelina a sympathetic smile.

"Please rest assured that we will do everything we can to keep your mother comfortable during surgery and throughout this round of treatments. I do want to warn you. She *is* going to be sicker this time, so I'll prescribe some stronger anti-nausea medications. This medicine will also be more expensive."

Angelina had the strangest sense of déjà vu, and then she remembered.

It wasn't the first time Dr. Campbell had given her that very same speech.

The city was stifling.

Maybe Dylan had grown accustomed to the serenity of the country, but downtown Nashville—with its noise and commotion—was like a shock to his system.

It was the last place on earth he wanted to be.

During the past four days, Dylan had struggled to concentrate. His mind was two hundred miles away, in a little town tucked in the heart of the Smoky Mountains. Numbly, he'd sat through countless meetings with his editor, trying his best to explain why he couldn't finish the article.

"Let me get this straight," Steve had said. "You're killing the feature because you've got the hots for this girl?"

"It's not quite that black and white, but yes."

Dylan's boss had been less than pleased, and when Steve made it clear he would write the article or find himself unemployed, Dylan had thanked him for his time and walked right out the door.

"Any luck?" his mom asked. The two of them were sitting in the living room. Patti was watching the news while Dylan scrolled through his phone, searching for a new job.

"Some freelance offers."

"Freelance wouldn't be a bad place to start," Patti said.

Dylan glanced up from his cell. His mom's brown eyes were soft as she smiled at her son. She'd been supportive about the entire situation, and he was thankful.

Patti Thomas gazed at her son. While she didn't completely understand why he had quit his job, she admired his resolve to follow his heart. When he had unexpectedly shown up on her doorstep, she'd known in an instant that something monumental had taken place on his assignment in the mountains. Desperate to talk to someone, Dylan had spilled his guts to his mom, and while she wasn't sure how she felt about this witchcraft business, she couldn't ignore the way his eyes lit up whenever he mentioned Angelina's name. Watching her son mope around for days had been strangely satisfying. He was talented and had always been passionate about his dreams to become a serious writer, but to see him head over heels for this woman definitely warmed her heart.

He was young, in love, and unemployed.

Patti tried not to dwell on that last detail. Besides, she had something important to share, and she had no idea how her son was going to react.

"I'm glad you're home, because I have some news."

Dylan glanced up from his phone. "Oh?"

"Charles called."

"Charles who?"

"Your father."

He snorted. "Well, that only took twenty years. Did you tell him to go to hell?"

"Yes, I did."

Dylan smiled. "Good for you."

"But then he called back. Three times. He works in publishing and saw one of your articles. He didn't go into details, and I didn't ask, but he was impressed with your work. He'd like to talk to you."

"I hope you told him there was no way in hell that was ever going to happen."

"I told him the decision was yours. You're an adult. This has to be your choice." Patti searched her son's face. "Aren't you at all tempted to hear what he has to say?"

"He left you penniless and me without a father. Why would I be interested in anything the man says?"

Patti nodded. "I understand that. I don't need your father's apology, but I think he owes you one. Besides, he's your dad, and I think you're just now realizing how important family can be."

"*You* are my family."

"You know what I mean."

Dylan couldn't deny that, since meeting Angelina and her mom, he'd come to value the sanctity of family. Still, it had taken his father two decades to reach out to him, and Dylan wasn't feeling very charitable.

"Will you at least think about it?" his mom asked.

"I don't want to think about it."

"But *will* you?"

Dylan sighed. "Fine, I'll think about it."

They said goodnight, and Patti headed upstairs while Dylan continued scrolling through his phone. There was a copy editor position open at an Asheville newspaper, and he mentally calculated the mileage between there and Maple Ridge.

Suddenly, he felt his chest tighten. It was the weirdest sensation, and his entire body froze. He inhaled sharply and tried to catch his breath as suffocating panic flowed through his veins.

Something's wrong.

"You're very quiet tonight," Celia said.

"Sorry."

The two of them were sitting on the couch. Celia was watching television while Angelina stared at the walls, feeling nothing but lost and alone. Cash was lying between them, with his head propped on her leg.

Angelina's mind was on a constant loop.

My mother has breast cancer.

Again.

Stupidly, foolishly, she had hoped the chemo would do its job. And now her mother was facing another surgery? Another round of treatments?

Would it make any difference whatsoever?

"Don't be sorry, Angelina. Just talk to me."

"What do you want me to say?"

"Whatever you want to say."

Her mother's patience was endless, but Angelina was too upset and far too bitter to have a rational conversation. The last thing she wanted to do was to make her mom feel guilty about something that was completely out of her control.

The only person Angelina could really talk to was hundreds of miles away.

Celia sighed. "I'm tougher than you think."

Angelina's father had told her the same thing—right here on this couch.

She took a breath.

She could be bitter later. She could cry later. Right now, she had to be strong for her mom.

"I know you're tough," Angelina said, trying to sound

brave. "I am, too, and I'll be right here, every step of the way. You know that, right?"

Her mother smiled. "I know you will."

It was late when they said goodnight. Before climbing into bed, Angelina checked her cell and noticed a text and several voice mails from Dylan. She wanted to call him. She *needed* to call him, but it was late. Besides, this news would have him speeding back to Maple Ridge, and as much as she needed him, she didn't want to be selfish.

Dylan needed time, and she would give it to him.

Rest didn't come easy. Angelina lay in bed for hours, tossing and turning. Her thoughts were jumbled and scared as she contemplated the possibility of a life without her mom. It was in her nature to be a cynic. Humans were imperfect, religion was complicated, and magic was complex, so the concept of faith was a tough one for Angelina. While she had inherited most of her mother's traits, Celia's unwavering sense of calm was the one quality her daughter failed to possess. Angelina would gladly trade her big blue eyes and mystical wisdom for an ounce of her mom's serenity.

There, in the darkness of her bedroom, Angelina finally allowed herself to cry.

Twelve

Angelina's bed was much too warm. She felt gentle fingertips against her cheek and opened her eyes, blinking sleepily as she focused on his face.

"Hi," she whispered, certain she was dreaming.

"Hi."

Dylan was lying next to her, with his cheek pressed against the pillow.

"You're here.

"I'm here."

"In my room."

"Yeah."

"In my bed."

He grinned. "Is that okay?"

It was more than okay. It was absolutely perfect.

"I'm so glad you're here. How did you get in?"

"Your mom. She was sitting out on the porch when I arrived."

Confused, Angelina turned her head, glancing at the

128

alarm clock on her nightstand.

"Mom was outside at three in the morning?"

"Yeah. She said she'd been waiting for me—whatever that means. There was an accident on I-40 or I would have been here hours ago."

So the psychic had a vision and failed to tell her daughter.

Thanks a lot, Mom.

"I didn't expect you until next week. Why'd you come back so early?"

"Because you needed me."

Their eyes remained locked on one another as he caressed her face.

"How did you know I needed you?"

"I was sitting in my mom's living room when I had this sudden, overpowering, suffocating need to see you. I'd missed you the entire time I was away, but *this* . . . this was so different. And then you didn't answer your phone. It terrified me, and I don't scare easily. But I *knew*. I knew you needed me, so here I am."

"I did need you," she admitted. "I mean, I *do*. I do need you."

"What's wrong?"

Angelina tried to blink back her tears, but they fell anyway as she told him about the doctor's diagnosis.

"I'm scared, and I'm bitter. I just . . . I don't understand cancer. I'll never understand it. They pump you full of poison for weeks and weeks, only for you to be told it didn't *work*? It didn't make one bit of difference? But we're going to do it again? Oh, and this time, you're going to be even *sicker*?"

Dylan pulled her close, and she buried her face

against his neck. She cried and cried until she was sure she had no more tears to shed. Then he would say something sweet and hold her a little tighter, and Angelina would just weep harder.

Eventually, her tears subsided, leaving her feeling shattered and drained.

"You should sleep," Dylan said. He kissed her forehead and started to rise from the bed.

Panic gripped her. "Where are you going?"

"Just to the couch, sweetheart. I can't check in at the motel until morning."

"I wish you'd stay. Stay here with me."

Dylan wanted that, more than anything.

"Are you sure? What about Celia?"

Angelina smiled for the first time in days. Dylan had no way of knowing that finding them in bed together— even if it was completely innocent—would be the highlight of her mother's year.

"She let you into my bedroom, didn't she?"

Dylan couldn't argue with that. He rose up just long enough to kick off his shoes before snuggling under the blanket. Angelina rested her head against his chest, and he buried his nose in her hair as his arms enveloped her.

"Celia's going to be okay," he murmured sleepily. Then he laughed. "It's too bad there aren't any psychic witches in your family. I bet if we had a crystal ball, we'd see that your mom is going to be just fine."

That was another thing he had no way of knowing. They *did* have a psychic in the family. And that's when Angelina realized that maybe her mother didn't possess some unwavering sense of calm after all. Perhaps Celia's serenity came from knowing she would, indeed, be okay.

Angelina felt a glimmer of hope swell in her heart, and she closed her eyes.

The morning sun beamed through her window. It was far too bright, and her eyes snapped open.

Am I late for work?

A set of strong arms tightened around her, pulling her back against his chest, and the shop was quickly forgotten. Smiling, Angelina snuggled deeper, tugging the blanket around them.

"You're beautiful, but you snore like a lumberjack," Dylan murmured against her ear.

A giggling Angelina slid her hand along his arm before linking their fingers together.

"I don't snore."

Dylan laughed softly and placed a kiss just below her ear.

"Good morning, baby."

She smiled, loving the endearment. "Good morning. This is nice."

"I was just thinking the same thing. Maybe I should move in."

"Maybe you should."

"Think Celia would mind?"

Angelina laughed. "Celia would be thrilled."

For a moment, she felt guilty for being so happy, knowing what her mother would soon be facing. Dylan sensed her change in mood, because he held her a little tighter, pressing a soft kiss against her neck.

"I really missed you, Angelina."

"I missed you, too."

"I thought a lot about what you said—about the spell

and how you're afraid to trust that my feelings are real. And I understand because I'm a skeptic, too. I believe in your healing touch, obviously, but I probably wouldn't have if I hadn't witnessed it. But *this* . . . what I feel for you . . . what I've felt for you since the moment I laid eyes on you. This is real, Angelina. I know it is."

"It's real for me, too," Angelina said, closing her eyes. "I needed you last night, and now you're here."

"And I knew you needed me. How crazy is that?"

Angelina delicately raked her nails against his arm, causing goose bumps to erupt against his flesh.

"It's very overwhelming," she said. Then her face split into a grin. "My mom is going to be thrilled. She's always believed that you came to Maple Ridge because I wished for you."

"Which is why she's been so adamant about the two of us getting along?" He chuckled. "That hurts a little. I thought she really liked me."

"She does, trust me. I might be an adult, but my mother would never have allowed you in my bedroom at three in the morning if she didn't *like* you."

"Well, that's reassuring. I couldn't believe she was sitting out on the porch last night. What do you think she meant when she said she'd been waiting for me?"

Angelina didn't want to lie to him, but her mother's gift was a story only she could share.

"You'll have to ask her about that. Are you always a reporter?"

Dylan stilled, and Angelina immediately detected the change in his mood.

What did I say?

"Not always, no," he murmured, nuzzling her.

Needing to be closer, Angelina reached behind her, drawing his leg over hers. She was equally relieved and disappointed to find he was still wearing his jeans.

"I bet it was uncomfortable sleeping in denim."

"It's even more uncomfortable now."

Angelina didn't have to ask why.

Grinning, she wiggled against him. Dylan groaned low against her ear, causing shivers to ripple up her spine.

"Don't tempt me, Angelina. We're in your mother's house."

"Are you always going to be the voice of reason? Because I can't lie, that's going to get old really fast."

With a playful growl, Dylan rolled over onto his back, pulling her on top of him. They laughed, and with their chests and hips pressed together, it was so easy for Angelina to forget she had to behave. She kissed him deeply, feeling every ounce of her doubt and fear slip away as they explored each other's mouths.

"Are you tempted?"

Dylan gripped her hips tightly. "You have no idea."

Wrong. Angelina had *some* idea, but as much as she loved lying in bed with him, she knew they should go say good morning to her mom.

Dylan realized it, too, and she was just about to climb out of bed when he tightened his hold on her waist.

"One more kiss," he whispered.

Angelina's blue eyes glittered with happiness before she leaned down, kissing him softly once more.

"Do you want more pancakes? More juice?"

Angelina stifled her laughter as she watched her mother refill Dylan's glass for the third time. Celia was smiling brightly this morning, and it didn't take a genius to figure out why.

"So, what are your plans for the rest of the day?" Celia asked the two of them.

Suddenly, Angelina remembered.

"I didn't expect you back so soon," she said to Dylan. "I've made plans with Maddie to look at wedding dresses tonight. I could try to get out of it, but . . ."

"No, it's okay. You should spend time with Maddie," Dylan said, smiling at her. He then turned to her mom. "Celia, I need to do a few things in town, but I'd like to talk to you later, if you're feeling up to it?"

"Of course. Anytime is fine."

After they helped with dishes, Angelina called the store to check in with Maddie. They'd sold two banjos and a guitar, which was a definite improvement in sales. Maddie was thrilled to hear that Dylan had returned early, and she even offered to postpone their trip to the bridal shop so Angelina could spend the evening with him. It was tempting, but Angelina was the maid of honor, and she had duties to fulfill.

"You don't look too happy about this shopping trip," Dylan said as they walked toward their vehicles.

"I'm not. Shopping for *anything* with Maddie is kind of like an Olympic event. I can only imagine how traumatizing looking at wedding dresses is going to be."

Dylan pulled her close, wrapping his arms around her waist. "Can I have you all to myself this weekend?"

"Do you want me all to yourself?"

"Yes, I do. Is that okay?"

Angelina grinned and rose on her tip-toes, kissing him tenderly.

"More than okay," she told him.

Later that afternoon, Dylan and Celia took a walk to the pond. Cash was right by their side, barking loudly at the squirrels as they scurried into the woods.

"This was your father's land?" Dylan asked.

Celia nodded and looped her arm through his. "And his father's."

"Angelina told me about your husband and the fish hook," he said with a grin. "Very smooth."

Celia laughed. "Samuel was very romantic."

"You miss him."

"Every day."

"Angelina misses him, too," Dylan replied. "It's hard for me to relate to that. I never really knew my dad, and I'm glad."

"Why glad?"

He sighed deeply. "My father wasn't a good husband. He walked out when I was three years old. My mom had to work two jobs to take care of us and put herself through school. She's much happier without him, but it was hard growing up."

"Have you ever considered searching for him?"

"I hadn't, but Mom just told me he's been in touch with her. He hasn't bothered calling in twenty years, and *now* he wants to talk to me?"

"Do you want to talk to him?"

"I want to punch him in the face," Dylan muttered, and Celia laughed. "No, I don't want to talk to him, but my mom thinks I should consider it. I don't know. Maybe I should thank him."

Celia looked puzzled. "Thank him?"

He nodded. "I have no real memories of the man, but he taught me everything I need to know about being a good husband and father. He was the perfect example of what *not* to do."

Once they reached the pond, the two of them sat down on the dock. Sunlight reflected against the water and a soft breeze danced in the air.

"I bet the mountains are pretty in the fall."

"They are," Celia replied, smiling at him. "Dylan, I don't think you brought me out here to talk about your dad or the mountains, did you?"

Dylan grinned. "No."

She patted his hand in encouragement.

"I love your daughter," he said. "I haven't told her so, but I do. She's worried that my feelings are being influenced by the spell, and maybe they are. But I don't care. I love her. She won't believe me . . . not yet, anyway. And I don't want to say the words until she's ready to hear them."

Celia nodded. "You know her so well. Angelina is very stubborn. So are you. It's why the two of you are perfect for each other. But I don't think you'll have to wait much longer to tell her how you feel."

Dylan looked at her quizzically. "Can I ask you a question?"

"Of course."

"Last night, when you met me out on the porch, you said you'd been waiting for me. What did you mean?"

Celia laughed. "Ah, the inquisitive reporter. I've been expecting that question."

He grinned. "Well?"

"I believe Angelina told you we have gifts."

"Yes, she's a healer."

"And I'm clairvoyant," she explained. "So was my mother."

"You have psychic visions?"

"I prefer to think of them as spiritual dreams, but yes. That's why I was expecting you last night, and that's why I've known from the day you arrived in Maple Ridge that you would fall in love with my daughter."

With every new bit of information, it was becoming easier for Dylan to suspend belief.

"Did you foresee I was going to need a new job?"

Celia looked surprised. "No. Why do you need a new job?"

"Because I quit the magazine. I told my editor I wasn't going to finish this story, and he told me to write it or else. I chose *else*."

She smiled. "*That* I did foresee."

"You did?"

"Yes, but it didn't take a psychic vision to figure it out. I knew eventually Angelina would become more important than your story. I wasn't too concerned. While our privacy is important to us, it isn't as if we're harboring any deep, dark secrets, and the stories I shared with you can easily be found in your research down at the library or from some of the more talkative folks in town. Rumors and gossip have swirled around us for generations, and people will choose to believe what they want to believe."

"But I have proof."

"Yes, when Angelina healed your hands," Celia said. "She is quite gifted. She always has been. Like most teenagers, she went through her period of rebellion, but in her case, she was rebelling against her natural instincts.

Angelina wanted to be normal, and that combined with her father's death, is why she doesn't practice magic. And that's her choice."

They grew quiet, giving Dylan the chance to absorb that information. After a few minutes, Celia turned to him.

"Now, I have a question for you."

"Shoot."

"You do realize you have a choice, too?" she said softly. "It's not as if the spell turns a man into a puppet on a string. Just because the spell brought you here doesn't mean you have to stay. That is *your* choice, Dylan."

He nodded thoughtfully, but he knew, deep in his heart, it wasn't really true.

He didn't have a choice at all.

Thirteen

Choosing Angelina's bridesmaid's dress had taken a grand total of fifteen minutes. The gown was pretty and purple, with a halter neckline. It was three hours later, and Maddie was trying on her tenth dress, thanks to an overly enthusiastic bridal consultant who was dying to make a hefty commission.

"I thought you wanted something simple?"

Maddie appraised herself in the full-length mirror. "You don't think this is pretty?"

"I think it's beautiful," Angelina said, peering at the ribbons in the back. "Is that a corset?"

Lydia, the consultant, shot her a disapproving glare, and Angelina glared right back.

"This is an organza ball gown with a chapel train," Lydia said as she began toying with the laces. "The veil is made of imported lace with scalloped edging. Any bride would love to walk down the aisle wearing this dress."

Lydia was getting on Angelina's nerves.

"It's a stunning gown, and you look gorgeous in it," Angelina told her best friend. This formal dress wasn't even close to what Maddie had described as wanting for her wedding day. Angelina worried she was going to fall in love with it and not be able to afford it. While Lydia continued her sales pitch, Angelina snuck a glance at the price tag.

No way.

No.

She had to get creative.

"While it makes you look fantastic, I bet that corset is a lot of work for the groom," Angelina said nonchalantly.

Maddie's head snapped up. "What do you mean?"

"I don't know. I was just thinking it might really kill the mood on your wedding night. You know, having to take the time to undo all these ribbons before the honeymoon can begin. Time that could be spent doing more important things . . ."

Maddie's face paled. "And Nick was never a Boy Scout. What if he can't get me unlaced?"

Angelina stifled a giggle.

Lydia could sense she was losing her commission. "Well, that's why you buy a going-away dress! You'll change at the church. I'm sure your bridesmaid will be happy to help you with the ribbons. We have some lovely—"

"I can't afford *two* dresses," Maddie snapped. "No, this won't work at all. I need something simple and classic. Easy on and *definitely* easy off."

Angelina managed to hide her smile as a disgruntled Lydia went off in search of dress number eleven. She began unstrapping her friend from the two thousand dollar dress, and when she looked up, she caught Maddie's eye in the mirror.

"Thank you," she mouthed.

Angelina winked.

"This corset really is a pain in the ass," she said, tugging on the ribbons.

Maddie smiled. "Thank you for being here."

"Of course. Where else would I be?"

"With your mom. With Dylan."

"I can be with them all weekend. This is important."

"She's going to be okay, you know," Maddie said. "This second round of chemo will do exactly what it's supposed to do."

Angelina nodded, not trusting herself to speak.

"I didn't think you were expecting Dylan until next week."

"I wasn't." The last of the laces fell away, and Maddie let the dress pool at her feet. "It was a complete surprise when he showed up in my bedroom this morning."

"In your bedroom?"

Angelina told her all about Dylan's arrival and her mother's premonition that he was coming.

"And she didn't tell you?" Maddie laughed just as Lydia arrived with another dress. "It's a good thing you don't sleep in the nude. Or maybe that's a *bad* thing . . ."

Imagining the two of them snuggling naked under a blanket caused butterflies to erupt in Angelina's stomach.

"It's a bad thing," she muttered.

Maddie giggled as Lydia helped her step into the dress. The gown was made of satin and lace, with no straps, no train, and—most importantly—no corset.

The girls gazed at the mirror.

"This is perfect," Maddie said.

Tears welled in Angelina's eyes, because it really was.

After choosing a simple veil and shoes, the girls were in the car and headed back to Maple Ridge. Maddie was in her bride bubble, chatting away about her ideas for the reception. As happy as Angelina was for her friend, her mind couldn't help but drift.

So much was happening right now. Her mother was scheduled for another surgery, she and Dylan were growing closer, and Maddie was getting married and moving away. There was such a mixture of happiness and sadness in Angelina's world.

Is this life? Moments filled with overwhelming joy and crippling misery? Taking the bitter with the sweet? Enjoying the rain because without it, you'd never see a rainbow? Are all of those annoying clichés really the secret to a happy life?

"You're thinking about your mom, aren't you?"

Angelina sighed and gazed out the window. "Among other things, but yeah."

"And Dylan?"

"And Dylan. And you."

"Well, your mom and I are going to be just fine," Maddie said with a smile. "And Dylan is absolutely crazy about you."

"I know. He told me."

"Did he?"

Angelina nodded. "I told him about the spell, too. He knows everything now."

"Does he believe in it?"

"He wasn't sure at first, which is absolutely the right response for a sane person to have," Angelina replied.

"Now that he's back, he says he doesn't care about the spell. That it doesn't matter."

"It doesn't. All that matters is how you make each other feel. Girls wait their whole lives and kiss a lot of frogs before finding their prince. So what if some ancient spell helped move things along? He's in love with you, Angelina. The only reason he hasn't told you is because he knows you won't believe him. It's going to be so much fun watching him prove it to you, and I hope he works quickly, because I don't want to miss a minute of it. *And* I can't wait until he sees you in that dress we bought tonight."

Angelina couldn't help but grin. Who would be her fountain of romantic optimism when Maddie moved away?

"Speaking of dresses, tell Nick he owes me. You looked so beautiful in it, but he would have *hated* unlacing that corset."

Maddie wrinkled her nose. "It was really uncomfortable, but I was willing to deal with it because it made my boobs look *so, so* good."

The girls laughed all the way home, and Angelina savored it, because she knew it could be one of the last times they'd have the chance. Maddie would be busy planning her wedding, and Angelina would be taking care of her mom after her surgery.

But for tonight, they were just two best friends, giggling like teenagers and talking about boobs and boys.

When Dylan asked if he could have Angelina all to himself for the weekend, she had no idea how lucky she would get. Celia was spending Saturday at a bluegrass festival in Strawberry Plains. It was only about an hour drive, but

Celia and her friend chose to spend the night at a hotel and drive back home on Sunday.

Angelina didn't ask the name of the friend, and in return, Celia didn't ask where Dylan would be sleeping on Saturday night.

Ignorance was bliss for all involved.

Angelina and Dylan were cuddled in her bed, pretending to watch a movie. Instead, they alternated kisses with conversation, and Dylan admitted he'd quit his job.

"But you loved your job."

"I love to write, but it wasn't as if I wanted to work there the rest of my life anyway. I have a few freelance offers. It'll be fine."

"So there's no article?" Angelina asked.

"No article."

Her face fell as emotion bubbled inside her. Without a story, Dylan had no reason to stay in Maple Ridge.

Everybody leaves.

"Hey, I thought you'd be happy about that. You never wanted me to write the feature."

"I know, but . . ." Her voice trailed off. She took a deep breath. "So, I guess you're . . . headed back to Nashville soon."

Dylan frowned. "Why would I be going back to Nashville?"

"There's no reason for you to stay."

Dylan rolled them over, pressing her into the mattress. Angelina snaked her arms around his neck, sighing softly when he rubbed his nose against hers.

"I think you're a very good reason to stay. The best reason."

Angelina moaned as he dipped his head, trailing his lips along her neck. His breath was warm against her skin, and she pulled him closer, desperate to anchor herself to him and never let him go. Instinctively, she arched against him, and he groaned, capturing her mouth with his once more.

When they finally pulled away, panting and breathless, Dylan pressed his forehead to hers.

"If I'm spending the night with you and sleeping in your bed, then you and I need to have a serious conversation."

Sighing heavily, Angelina framed his face with her hands. "I'm so tired of serious conversations. For one night, can't we just do whatever we feel like doing and ignore the rest?"

He chuckled and rolled over onto his back. Groaning, Angelina turned onto her side and gazed down at the infuriating man lying beside her.

"Don't you want me?" Her voice was timid.

With a hungry look in his eyes that made her tremble, Dylan reached for her, pulling her face down to his. Angelina whimpered into his mouth, clutching his shirt in her hand. She let her fingers slide beneath the fabric, and he whispered a curse when she brushed her nails across his stomach. His low groan gave her courage, and within seconds, his shirt was gone. Feeling brave, she eagerly reached for the zipper of his jeans.

"Baby," he murmured, his hand gripping hers. "If you value my sanity at all, you won't do that."

Angelina buried her face against his neck. *Why does he have to be a nice guy? Why?*

But deep down, she knew she wouldn't want him any

other way. It wasn't rejection she felt. It was confusion, and maybe, a little embarrassment. Dylan wanted her—she had no doubt about that—and they had this big house all to themselves for the night.

What was he waiting for?

"Do you know how much I care about you?" Dylan whispered against her ear. "Do you know how much it would kill me if you regretted this?"

"I care about you, too." The words sounded so wrong. Almost blasphemous. Because she *more* than cared about him. "And I wouldn't regret it."

Gazing up at her, he smiled and pushed a strand of hair behind her ear.

"You told me you're a virgin."

"Yes, I am."

"Why?"

"Why am I a virgin?"

He nodded and gently brushed his hand against her cheek. "Don't get me wrong. I love that you are. I'm just curious as to why. I mean, you've waited for a reason, and I don't want to be the jerk that comes along and makes you regret not waiting a little longer."

"I don't want to wait any longer."

"But why did you wait at all? Were you saving yourself for marriage or . . ."

She shook her head. "No. I mean, it's a noble goal, but that isn't why I've waited."

"Then why, Angelina?"

She took a deep breath.

"Because a very small piece of my heart still believed in the spell. I wanted to wait . . . for him. Just in case."

Dylan couldn't hide his smile. "So you *do* believe in

magic."

She shrugged and lowered her head, letting her hand trail across his inked bicep. "I'd forgotten you have a tattoo."

Angelina ghosted her fingers along the black ink. The design was two crisscrossed drumsticks with a half-heart in the middle.

"You must have really loved playing drums," she said.

"I did, yeah."

"Not anymore?"

"It was never a real passion. Just more of a phase. My mother was relieved when it finally passed."

Angelina giggled. "The drumsticks I understand, but why the half-heart?"

"It was symbolic."

"Of?"

Dylan shrugged. "I don't know. It could mean a lot of things, I guess."

She wasn't letting him off that easy. "It must have meant something to you."

Dylan sighed. "My mom seemed to think it symbolized my feelings about my dad. He left me incomplete, or some bullshit like that."

"You don't agree with her?"

"My father was the last thing on my mind when I picked the design. I just thought it looked cool and represented my life at the time. You know, like maybe I was this imperfect and unfinished beating heart. I was nineteen years old. Still growing up and trying to decide what I wanted to do with my life."

With a smile, Angelina gently traced the outline of the heart with her fingertip. "I love that."

Dylan shuddered as her hand traveled down his arm and along his chest.

"What's this?" she asked, running her finger along a spot just above his navel.

"I had chicken pox when I was ten." Dylan held his breath when she dipped her head to press a soft kiss against the scar. "Can you heal it?"

Angelina smiled against his skin. "I don't know. I've never tried healing old wounds. I wouldn't want to, anyway. It's part of who you are. Some scars are good, I think. They remind you of where you've been."

Her voice was soft and quiet, and he couldn't help but wonder if she had any scars of her own.

"Did you ever have chicken pox?"

Angelina laughed. "No. Anytime we had an epidemic at school, mom would conjure some kind of potion to protect me. Magic sometimes has its advantages. I have a tattoo, though."

Suddenly, he sat up in bed and reached for her, pulling her into his lap so they were nose-to-nose.

"Show me," he murmured roughly.

She grinned and wrapped her arms around his neck. "Are you trying to distract me from wanting to have sex?"

"Maybe a little."

"Then showing you mine is probably a very bad idea. I'd have to be naked for you to really get the full effect."

Dylan groaned and buried his face against her neck. They held each other close until Angelina finally whispered against his ear.

"Why do you want to wait?"

He lifted his head and found himself staring into her confused blue eyes.

"Because I love you," he said simply. "I want to wait because I love you."

Angelina gasped.

"You love me?"

Dylan rubbed his nose against hers. "You know I do. You just don't believe it in your heart. Not yet. And that's why I want to wait."

He kissed her deeply, and Angelina moaned into his mouth. Tightening her arms around his neck, she pressed herself against him, desperate to have him closer as she savored his sweet words.

"I love you," he whispered, letting his lips linger against her cheek.

Angelina wanted to say it back, but the words hung in her throat, suffocating her. Dylan placed his hands on each side of her face, forcing her to look into his eyes.

"Don't say it, Angelina. Not tonight."

Her eyes flashed with confusion. "You don't want me to say it?"

"Oh, I want you to say it. I just want you to mean it. I want you to be sure. I don't want there to be an ounce of fear or doubt in your heart when you say those words to me."

She pressed her forehead to his.

"There won't be," she promised him.

Fourteen

The morning of her mom's surgery was rainy and cool—a perfect complement to Angelina's mood. Celia, in her white hospital gown, was her usual serene self as they sat in the pre-op room. Dylan had insisted on coming along, and Celia had agreed, knowing Angelina would need support today.

"How can you be so calm about this?" Angelina asked.

Dylan slid his hand along the nape of her neck and caressed the skin there. Her anxiety was at a fever pitch, and he was doing everything in his power to keep her calm.

"Because worrying won't change a thing," Celia said quietly. "You know that better than anyone. We just have to let the surgeon do his job."

Angelina needed a little grain of hope to hang onto before they wheeled her mother back to surgery. Now that

Dylan was aware of her mom's visions, she didn't hesitate to ask her next question.

"What have you *seen?*" she asked nervously.

Before Celia could answer, Dr. Campbell walked into the room with the surgeon.

As the introductions were made, Dylan kept a tight grip on Angelina's trembling hand. He seriously considered asking the doctor for something to relax her, because he had no idea how he was going to keep her calm during her mom's two-hour surgery. The doctors talked to them about anesthesia and recovery exercises, but it was all white noise to Dylan. All he could concentrate on was the woman he loved, quivering at his side.

When the nurse announced it was time, Angelina carefully hugged her mom, promising her they would be waiting when she woke up. When it was Dylan's turn, Celia pulled him close.

"I'm trusting you to take care of her," Celia whispered in his ear.

Dylan nodded numbly.

For the next two hours, he did everything he could to keep Angelina's mind off the surgery, but it was pointless. They were sitting in a hospital, surrounded by sick kids and crying families, and there was no way to ignore any of it. He watched helplessly as Angelina paced the room like a caged lion. Her eyes were red and her cheeks were wet, and there was nothing he could do.

It killed him.

After an hour had passed, Dylan finally took her by the hand.

"Let's get some fresh air."

Angelina shook her head. "I'm not leaving."

"Just out those doors," he said, pointing toward the sliding glass. "We won't go far, I promise."

She nodded, and he led her outside. They found a bench close by, and Dylan pulled her close to his side. Angelina went willingly, resting against him as he enveloped her in his arms. He kissed her hair and wished he could promise that everything was going to be fine, but he didn't dare, because he didn't know.

And the not knowing was the toughest part of all.

"Angelina, stop hovering. I'm fine."

It wasn't the first time Angelina had heard those words, and she knew it wouldn't be the last.

"You look uncomfortable," Angelina mumbled, reaching behind her mom and adjusting the pillow. Finally satisfied, she settled herself on the couch next to her. The two of them were watching some cooking show on television. That, combined with the smell of garlic streaming from the kitchen, made Angelina's stomach growl for the first time in days.

It had been one week since her mom's surgery. Dr. Campbell had deemed the operation a success and sent them home three days later with illustrated instructions and enough medications to open a small pharmacy. Thankfully, Celia's surgical drain had been removed before she had been discharged, so that was a relief.

Maddie took care of the store while Angelina focused on her mother's recovery. She helped Celia with her arm exercises, made sure she took her medication when needed, and refused to let her mom lift a finger. Celia was tired most of the time, which was to be expected, but Angelina could tell she was growing restless. She tried her best to keep her mom entertained, but Celia wasn't used to sitting around the house.

"Something smells good," Celia said.

"Dylan's making spaghetti for lunch."

Her mom grinned. "That boy should just move in."

Angelina smiled, because it was true. He practically lived there already, doing everything in his power to take care of the two of them.

"David is coming over this afternoon," Celia said. "I want you and Dylan to get out of this house for a while, and I want no argument from either of you. Dr. Campbell warned you about focusing on my recovery and neglecting to take care of yourself. It's been a week. I want the two of you to go into town, check on the store, and do something besides sit here with me."

Her mother's voice was firm, and Angelina knew better than to argue.

"Do you think she's okay?"

Dylan squeezed her hand as they walked along the sidewalk. "I think she'll be fine, and if she isn't, David will call us."

Angelina nodded and tried to focus on anything but the anxiety bubbling in her stomach. Dylan did his best to distract her as he pointed toward the windows of the shops in town, and she smiled and pretended everything was right in the world.

"I know what you need," Dylan said, pulling her toward a picnic table just outside of Fay's Bakery. She sat down, and he leaned close, kissing her forehead. "Stay here. I'll be right back."

He walked into the shop, and Angelina closed her

eyes, inhaling the fresh mountain air. Her nerves were shot, and while she understood that worry was a useless emotion, she couldn't help but feel uneasy each and every time she saw her mom's tired face. In many ways, surgery was the easy part. Next would come the punishing chemo, and with that, Celia's body would have to tolerate the crippling nausea and enormous fatigue. Angelina prayed she would be strong enough to help her mom endure all of it.

The tinkling of the bakery door resonated in her ears, and Angelina opened her eyes. She couldn't help but smile as Dylan walked back to the picnic table, holding two cupcakes in his hands.

"How did you know I love Fay's strawberry cupcakes?"

"Wild guess," Dylan said as he sat down, straddling the bench.

Angelina turned toward him, their knees brushing against each other as they sat as close as possible. He kissed her softly before handing her a cupcake.

"Thank you."

"For what?"

"For taking such good care of me and my mom."

Dylan smiled. "Thank you for letting me. I'm just thankful both of you had an appetite this afternoon."

"Me, too."

While they ate their cupcakes, Dylan told Angelina about a call he'd received from a Knoxville newspaper, offering him some freelance work.

"It's just mainly fluff pieces," he said with a shrug. "But at least I won't have to travel as much."

"But you like to travel."

"I do, but now is not the time. I'll travel later. Right now, I need to be here."

Angelina sighed. She hated the thoughts of him giving up anything just to stay in Maple Ridge and take care of her.

"Hey," he whispered, tilting her face toward his. "I *want* to be here. There's no place else I'd rather be. Never doubt that."

His voice rang with sincerity, and she smiled before leaning in, kissing him tenderly. When she pulled away, she rested her hand against his chest.

"Your heart's racing."

"Your fault."

Angelina giggled.

"I've missed your laugh, baby."

"I've missed laughing."

Dylan kissed her forehead. "Why don't we go see Maddie? Talking about the wedding is sure to brighten your mood."

"You brighten my mood every single day. Never doubt that."

Dylan smiled.

Over the next few weeks, their lives slowly returned to a somewhat normal routine. Celia began her treatments, and as Dr. Campbell predicted, the chemo combined with the medications kept her sick most of the time. Despite her desire to spend every moment by her mom's side, Angelina had reluctantly returned to work at the shop. David Murray had offered to stay with Celia, and he would check in with Angelina throughout the day. Dylan began his freelance work with the newspaper in Knoxville and found a tiny apartment in town. Maddie was knee-deep in wedding plans, and with the ceremony only a week away, she kept Angelina distracted with her maid of honor responsibilities.

The distraction worked, until the evening Angelina returned home to find Celia slumped over the sofa, retching into a garbage can.

Dylan was right by her side, holding her hair.

Sadly, watching her mother vomit wasn't anything new, but seeing Dylan taking such good care of her mom brought tears to Angelina's eyes. In that moment, she was finally grateful for the magic spell that had brought such a wonderful man into their lives.

The next day, Dylan dropped Angelina off at the store before heading to the coffee shop. As he stood in line, he tiredly rubbed his face and wondered how a man's life could change so dramatically in such a short period of time.

How long had he been living in Maple Ridge? He was too tired to do the math, but he was sure it had only been a couple of months. And in that time, he'd lost his job, been tossed into jail, and had fallen in love with the woman of his dreams.

Dylan smiled every time he thought of her, and he knew without a doubt that *this* was where he was meant to be. He was tempted to find a tattoo parlor and have the artist fill in the rest of his heart.

His life no longer felt incomplete.

Dylan was still smiling when his cell vibrated in his hand. Glancing down at the screen, he noticed it was an email from Beth, his editor at the newspaper, asking Dylan to come by the office the next day. The paper's editor-in-chief—a guy by the name of Chuck—had apparently been impressed with Dylan's freelance work and wanted to offer him a full-time position.

Excited for the opportunity and steady paycheck, he quickly typed out a reply, promising Beth he would be there at ten, just as Chuck had requested.

He couldn't believe his luck. Knoxville was only an hour away, and it was another sign that moving to Maple Ridge was the right decision.

Dylan was excited to have some good news to share with Angelina and her mom because the past few weeks had been rough on all of them. Celia's body was still adjusting to the treatments and medications. She was trying to be strong for Angelina, and it had finally taken its toll. Angelina had cried all night long, and he'd held her close, whispering he loved her, and that he would be by her side through it all.

But he couldn't deny he was tired.

So tired.

And his exhaustion was making him irritable, so when he overheard two guys in the coffee line talking about the pretty owner of the music store next door, he found it difficult to keep his temper in check.

"We dated back in high school," one of the guys said. Dylan recognized the man's face but couldn't remember his name.

Angelina's first date. Kyle something?

"Oh yeah? What was she like?" his friend asked.

The man didn't even bother to whisper.

"Hands down, the best sex of my life."

The guys paid for their coffee, and they were still

laughing as they walked right past him on their way to the door.

Dylan was tired and cranky, and the last thing he needed was to hear some asshole spreading bullshit about the woman he loved.

Caffeine was no longer important.

He didn't even think about the consequences of his actions. Didn't even consider that this was probably a very bad idea.

He didn't think at all.

Dylan turned on his heel and followed the men out the door.

Angelina gazed across the water, watching the sun dip just below the trees. Cash was by her side, snuggling close. Each time she was sure she was all cried out, a fresh wave of tears would fall.

What was he thinking? Isn't life chaotic enough without him getting into another brawl—and this time, in the middle of town?

She had refused to bail him out this time. Despite that, the thought of him sitting in a cold jail cell was more than she could bear. On the phone, he'd begged her to forgive him. Pleaded with her to understand. But all she could see in her mind was his fist connecting with Kyle Dobb's jaw, and that visual brought to mind another boyfriend who couldn't keep his rage under control.

Angelina couldn't live that way again.

She wouldn't.

It was nearly dark when Cash's ears perked, and Angelina knew she had company. Minutes later, she felt his arm brush against hers as he joined her on the grass.

Angelina's eyes remained on the pond. "Who bailed

you out?"

"Maddie."

Angelina nodded stiffly.

"I know you're mad at me, but in my defense, you don't know what he said about you."

Angelina closed her eyes and sighed deeply. "My mother has cancer."

"You think I don't realize that?"

Angelina turned to face him. "If you realize that, then you should also realize I don't give a shit what Kyle Dobbs says about me. Kyle Dobbs is not important to me. My mother is important. Maddie is important. You are important. Kyle Dobbs—and what he says about me—is at the very bottom of my list of important things."

Dylan stared down at his hands. "I know it was a stupid thing to do, but I love you. I am always going to be protective of you. I won't apologize for that."

She shook her head. "I can't handle this level of protectiveness. I can't keep waiting for a call from the sheriff to come bail you out of jail because you've punched someone in the face for saying something about me. People are going to talk, Dylan. They've talked about my family for generations."

Dylan scrubbed his face. "The last thing I want to hear while I'm waiting for coffee is that asshole telling his buddy how good you are in bed."

Angelina laughed. "Which you know is a lie because you know I'm a virgin! Don't you see? You got into a fight over nothing. You got tossed into jail—*again*—over nothing! I lived through one possessive boyfriend, and I won't do it again. I won't."

Dylan's jaw clenched.

"Don't compare me to him. I am nothing like Adam McDonald. I would never hurt you, Angelina. Never."

She knew, deep in her soul, Dylan would never raise his hand to her. She knew that. But his anger still scared her, and until he found a way to control his temper . . .

"I need some time to think," Angelina whispered shakily.

He closed his eyes. "How much time?"

"I don't know."

"Angelina, don't do this. I'll . . . work on my temper. I'll try. Just don't shut me out. "

She climbed to her feet.

"You're welcome to stay out here as long as you like. I'm going to go check on my mom."

Dylan bowed his head, and with her dog by her side, Angelina made her way back to the house.

Fifteen

The next morning, Dylan sped along the interstate on his way to Knoxville. He was thankful it was early and state troopers seemed to be few and far between. He was irritable and exhausted, and this was the absolute worst day to have an interview, but this job opportunity was too important to pass up.

Angelina was mad at him now, but that didn't weaken his resolve. His life was in Maple Ridge, and he needed to secure a steady job close to home if he had any chance of building a future with her.

If she ever forgives me.

He spent the hour drive contemplating how he was going to convince her to do just that, and by the time Dylan stepped into the offices of *The Knoxville Times*, he was crankier than ever.

The friendly receptionist smiled at him. "Good morning. May I help you?"

"Good morning. I have a job interview with the editor-in-chief."

"Your name?"

"Dylan Thomas."

The young woman giggled as she checked her computer screen.

"What a coincidence. You even look a little like him. Must be the eyes. Who knows? Maybe that'll help you land the job."

Dylan had no idea was she meant, and he was in no mood for riddles.

The receptionist pointed him toward the elevators. He thanked her as he walked away.

"Now I know what she meant by a coincidence," Dylan muttered under his breath as his eyes lingered on the editor-in-chief's name on the door.

Charles Thomas.

Chuck.

Charles.

It was, without a doubt, the biggest coincidence in the history of the world.

He hoped.

Because if it wasn't, and if the man sitting behind that desk was indeed Charles Thomas—the same Charles Thomas who'd left Dylan and his mom without a penny to their names all those years ago . . .

Dylan didn't know if he'd be able to control his temper.

How many times can one be arrested in a twenty-four-hour period?

Before he completely lost his nerve, he took a deep

breath and gently rapped on the door.

"Come in."

There was nothing familiar about the man's voice, but that did little to quell Dylan's anxiety. After all, his father had left when he was three. He wasn't sure he'd even recognize the man's face, let alone the sound of his voice.

Dylan took a deep breath, turned the door knob, and stepped inside.

The man behind the desk lifted his head, and Dylan found himself staring into a set of deep brown eyes.

His brown eyes.

"We do look alike. Patti said you were a carbon copy of me when I was your age, but—"

Dylan let the door slam behind him as Charles quickly rose to his feet.

An eerie silence filled the room as father and son examined each other for the first in twenty years. Charles Thomas's hair was streaked with gray, but there was no denying the person standing behind the desk was Dylan's father. The eyes were the same. The height was the same. Even their posture was the same. Both men were standing with their hands fisted at their sides.

"Is this a joke?"

Charles looked puzzled. "A joke?"

"I'm waiting for Ashton Kutcher to jump out and tell me I'm being punked."

"I don't think he hosts that show anymore."

"Like I give a shit what you think."

Charles sighed heavily and dropped back down into his chair. "Look, son—"

Dylan snorted. "You didn't seriously just call me your son, did you? Because you gave up the right to call me *anything* the day you walked out on me and my mom."

"I know you hate me, but if you'll just sit down and let me explain—"

"I don't want your explanation!"

"Maybe you don't want my explanation, but you want a job, don't you? I can help you with that. There's no money in freelance. I spoke with your mother a few days ago."

"Yeah, she told me. You can stop calling her, by the way. She doesn't want to listen to your crap any more than I do. And why all of a sudden are you so interested in me? You haven't been for the past twenty years, and I've done just fine without you."

Charles rubbed the back of neck. "That's . . . actually what I want to talk to you about. I need to make it right. I need to fix it before it's too late."

"It's already too late. You left my mother without a dime to her name. You left me without a father. I have absolutely nothing to say to you, and I wouldn't work for you or your newspaper if you begged me."

The two men stared daggers at each other.

Dylan knew he should turn on his heel and walk right out the door, but something was keeping him rooted to his spot. Maybe it was the sheer shock of coming face-to-face with his dad after so many years. Maybe it was just morbid curiosity.

"I'm in a position to help you," Charles told his son. "You'll starve doing freelance for this paper. You're a good writer, Dylan. I've seen your articles. Your future in journalism could be very bright."

Dylan's hand was already on the door knob. "*Could* be? Meaning, if I don't accept your help, I don't have a chance at all?"

"That's not what I meant," Charles muttered. "Give me five minutes. Forget I'm your father for five minutes and listen to what I have to say."

He laughed. "Forget you're my father for five minutes? Shouldn't be too hard. After all, you managed it for twenty years."

Charles exhaled a noisy sigh.

"Five minutes, Dylan."

"Fine."

Dylan dropped into the nearest chair.

Charles cleared this throat, and suddenly, he was all business.

"First of all, let me say your writing is impressive. Your freelance pieces have received some wonderful feedback from our readers. Your editor, Beth, says you have a killer work ethic, and you come highly recommended by Steve Jenkins. While you left him in a tight spot when you refused to write your feature, he says he couldn't help but be impressed that you stood your ground. He didn't go into detail as to why you quit, and I didn't ask. Maybe that's a story you'll tell me someday."

Dylan said nothing, although it was nice to hear that Steve didn't hate his guts.

"We need a columnist. Someone who likes to write human interest stories. From what I've gathered, that's your strength. People share their stories with you because they trust you. They have faith that you'll be professional and honest."

Dylan glanced down at his watch.

Three minutes.

"It's my understanding you've fallen in love . . . with

this area of the state," Charles remarked, smirking a little. "Your mom is under the impression you'd like to live close to the mountains. A full-time position here would allow for that. There would be some travel involved, obviously, but it'd be local. Perhaps some regional, depending on the season, but you'd never be far from home. How does that sound?"

Despite his aggravation—with both his father and his chatty mom—he couldn't deny it sounded pretty good. He could live in Maple Ridge, write full-time, and build a future with Angelina.

Dylan couldn't believe this messed-up, twisted universe. His first solid job opportunity, practically his dream job, and it was being offered to him by the man he hated most in this world.

"I can't believe you're the editor-in-chief of this newspaper."

Charles grinned. "I can't believe you're a writer. You know what they say. The apple doesn't fall far from the tree."

It was the wrong thing to say, and Dylan jumped to his feet, his eyes flashing with anger.

"I am in love with an amazing woman, and I can't stand to be away from her for more than a few hours at a time. You had a *wife*, and you deserted her. I am *nothing* like you."

And with that, Dylan stalked out of the room, slamming the door behind him.

So much for controlling my temper.

Once he was back in his car, he leaned his forehead against the steering wheel and tried to control his breathing.

Dylan never expected to see his father ever again. He had hoped, of course. Every birthday. Every Christmas. Dylan had spent most of his childhood wondering if this would be the year Charles Thomas returned to the family he had left behind. But years passed, and Dylan had accepted that his father was never coming back. With acceptance came a sense of peace that had followed him all these years.

And now that peace was shot to hell.

Dylan fished his cell phone out of his pocket. He knew she was mad and would probably let his call go straight to voice mail, so he sent her a text instead

I need my best friend.

When Angelina arrived at the house, she was surprised to find her mother sitting outside in her rocking chair. Dylan's SUV was parked in the driveway, but he was nowhere to be found.

How dare he send me some mysterious text message and scare the crap out of me!

Angelina ran toward the porch. "Where is he?"

"He took Cash down to the pond," Celia replied. "I know you're upset with him, but he needs you. He's stood by you—by *us*—so many times. It's your turn."

"Is he okay?"

"He will be."

Angelina couldn't handle any more cryptic messages, so she turned and sprinted toward the pond. Dylan was there, sitting on the grass. Her dog was lying next to him with his head perched in his lap.

He looks okay, she thought, and she felt her body relax, just a little, as she approached the water.

"I think you love this pond more than I do," Angelina said as she sat down next to him.

"Hi, sweetheart."

"Hey."

Dylan gazed across the water as he ran his fingers through Cash's coat. "I do love it here. You can sit and listen to the birds and watch the water ripple with the breeze. It's serene and calm. And that's what I want. I want peace and tranquility in a world that is so completely screwed up."

His tone was soft but cold, and it made Angelina wonder if there wasn't more on his mind than just their argument from last night. Her suspicions were confirmed when he reached for her hand.

"I know you're mad at me, but right now, I need to talk to my best friend. That's why I'm here, even though you asked me to stay away."

"I'm sorry I asked you to stay away. I don't want that."

"You don't?"

Angelina shook her head, and he smiled.

A nearby frog caused Cash to awaken from his nap, and he jumped up, bolting straight toward the water. With him out of the way, Angelina moved closer. Relieved to have the contact, Dylan lowered his head, nuzzling her shoulder.

"What's wrong?"

Dylan sighed heavily. "I had a job interview in Knoxville today."

"That's amazing! I didn't know you had an

interview."

"I didn't get the chance to tell you before . . . my latest arrest."

Angelina squeezed his hand. "How'd it go?"

"Horrifically. The editor-in-chief is my father."

Angelina's eyes widened.

"What are the odds, right?" Dylan chuckled, but there wasn't a hint of humor in his tone. "He offered me a job. A full-time position as a columnist."

"That's . . . incredible."

"Of course, he never got around to officially offering it to me. He said something about me being just like him, and I—"

She closed her eyes. "And you lost your temper."

"Yeah. And it's something I have to work on. I know this. But to hear him compare the two of us . . . it just enraged me, Angelina. I'm *nothing* like him. I would never abandon my family."

"I know you wouldn't."

"Do you?" Dylan asked, his voice laced with uncertainty as he gazed into her bright blue eyes. "Do you know I'd never desert you? I'd never deliberately hurt you? It doesn't matter if the spell is designed to keep me devoted and faithful. I am not Nathaniel Rose. I am not Adam McDonald, and I am most certainly not Charles Thomas. I know I'm not perfect, but I would never . . . I could never . . ."

"I know."

It was overwhelming, the need to be as close to him as she could possibly be. Without thinking twice, Angelina crawled into his lap, and Dylan enveloped her in his arms. His eyes flickered to her mouth, and she leaned in, kissing him softly.

"Don't be mad at me," he murmured.

"I'm not mad."

He smiled against her lips—his first honest smile all day—before kissing her once more.

"Am I really your best friend?" Angelina asked.

"Yes, you are. Not that I have many friends back home. I worked crazy hours and was always on the road. But yeah, you're my best friend. Isn't that how it's supposed to be when you love someone?"

Angelina thought of her parents. They'd definitely been best friends throughout their marriage. She'd always wanted that kind of love, and now she had it.

"Yes, that's how it should be."

Dylan rubbed his nose against hers. "I hate when we fight."

"Me, too."

They held each for a while until she finally asked what he was going to do about his father.

"I don't know," Dylan admitted with a sigh. "The job opportunity is incredible. I just don't know that I can stand working for him."

"I understand, but even if you don't accept the job, what will you do? Obviously, he wants to get to know you."

"He had his chance to get to know me. He blew it."

Angelina's eyes softened, and he couldn't ignore the sadness there.

"You think I should?"

She shook her head. "I can't answer that. You just . . . you don't know what I'd give to have one more conversation with my father. Just one. Your dad is offering you a dream job. He didn't have to do that, and I think it proves that he wants to try to make amends. Family is so important. You could wake up tomorrow and he'd be gone forever, and you would have missed your chance. I can't tell you what to do, but I do think you should think about it."

Dylan pressed his forehead to hers.

"Okay, I'll think about it."

She smiled, and they sat in a comfortable silence as they watched Cash chase frogs around the pond. He never caught them, but whether that was because the frogs were much too fast or because Cash just enjoyed the chase was a mystery.

Angelina played with the hair along the nape of his neck. "I know it's been a crazy day, but I need to ask you something."

"You can ask me anything."

"I need a date for Maddie's wedding. Interested?"

Dylan chuckled. "Very interested. Do I need a tux?"

"Nope, just a suit is fine," she said, smiling. "They've rented a chapel in Gatlinburg and reserved a block of rooms at one of the hotels for the guests. Mom isn't up to making the trip, so I was thinking we should tell Maddie we need . . . a room."

Dylan grinned.

Room.

Singular.

His hold tightened around her waist. He was far too excited as to where this conversation might be leading.

"I would be honored to be your date, and I think a *room* is a very good idea."

Neither said it, but both were thinking the exact same

thing.

This wedding was going to be a monumental occasion for one happy couple.

And it wasn't the bride and groom.

sixteen

Candlelight shimmered along the altar, casting a soft glow inside the mountain chapel. Maddie had wanted a small ceremony, so the tiny church was the perfect solution to seat the thirty friends and family who'd been invited to the wedding.

At the bride's request, Angelina was standing in the shadows in the back of the chapel, checking to see if the groom had arrived. Nick was easy to find—standing at the altar with his brother and the minister. His smile was wide and nervous as he fidgeted with his tie.

Angelina couldn't resist scanning the crowd, and her pulse quickened when she spotted Dylan sitting in the second row.

Tonight was the night.

Neither of them had verbalized it, but over the past few days—and with the promise of a weekend all to themselves—their kisses and touches had become more passionate than ever.

Angelina was nervous, absolutely, but there wasn't a doubt in her mind that this man was the one.

And tonight, she would tell him.

And show him.

Focus, Angelina. You have duties to fulfill.

Taking a deep breath, Angelina made her way back to the little dressing room and found the bride standing in front of the full-length mirror, adjusting her veil. While the maid of honor was a bundle of nerves, the bride was calm and serene as Felicia, the wedding coordinator, darted around the room in her pencil skirt and five-inch heels, barking orders into her cell phone. That was another great thing about using the Gatlinburg chapel. The wedding details that normally drove a bride insane—the flowers, the reception, and even the photographer—were all handled by the staff. All Maddie had to do was show up in her dress and make sure Nick arrived at the church on time.

"He's out there," Angelina confirmed with a grin.

Maddie's smile was bright. "How does he look?"

"Nervous. Handsome."

Maddie sighed happily and gazed at herself in the mirror. "You're next, you know."

"Next?"

"All of this," Maddie said, waving toward the flowers and the dress. "You're next."

"Hmm. I don't know about that."

"Please. He loves you. You love him. It's time you told him, by the way. I know you hate his temper, but good grief, he's allowed to have a flaw. Don't let one stupid imperfection ruin all of the other perfect moments that made you fall in love with him. He loves you, Angelina. He loves your mom. He will be faithful and devoted and treat you like a princess. That's what you wanted when you cast the spell, wasn't it? Your very own Prince Charming?"

Angelina nervously glanced around the room, but Felicia was too preoccupied with wedding drama to hear their crazy conversation.

"Sorry," Maddie whispered.

"It's okay, and you can stop now. I've already forgiven him."

Her face brightened. "You have?"

"I have. We're good."

Maddie's eyes flashed with mischief. "I did notice you only requested the one room."

"Well, it seemed like the . . . economical thing to do."

The bride snorted. "Whatever. I want *all* the details."

Angelina rolled her eyes, and the girls giggled.

"Wow, it's going to be a special night for both of us," Maddie said, her voice filled with awe. "Everything really is changing, isn't it?"

Angelina reached for Maddie's veil and gently toyed with the lace. "Yes, but these are good changes. Growing up. Falling in love. Finding your soul mate."

"We're so lucky, Angelina."

A brief look passed between the lifelong friends, and they immediately erupted into sobs.

"Are we ready?" Felicia asked brightly, but her face turned ashen when she saw their tears. She grabbed a box of tissues from the nearby table. "Okay, tell me what's wrong, and I'll tell you how we'll fix it."

Both girls laughed as they dried their eyes.

"We're just happy," Maddie promised her.

Felicia's shoulders sagged with relief, grateful there wasn't a wedding-related tragedy.

"Well, that's what we want! Happy bride. Happy maid of honor. Happy groom. Speaking of which, Nick looks as if he's a nervous wreck, but I've never seen a happier man standing at the altar. Are you ready to see him?"

"I'm ready," Maddie said, her voice strong and calm.

The three of them made their way toward the tiny sanctuary. A mandolin played the soft strains of "Canon in D" as Angelina took her place at the back of the aisle. She stared down at her purple and cream bouquet, took a long steadying breath, and began to walk. Angelina fixed her eyes on the altar as she followed the path of rose petals, and when she finally reached Nick and the minister, she lifted her head and turned toward the congregation.

In an instant, Angelina's eyes locked with Dylan's, and her breath hitched in her throat. He looked handsome, dressed in his dark suit and skinny tie. His eyes swept over her, and she felt a rush of excitement as his burning gaze never left hers—not even when the music changed, signaling everyone to stand.

Taking another deep breath, Angelina forced herself to look toward the aisle, where her glowing best friend was making her way toward the altar. Her arm was looped through her father's, and when they reached the minister, Maddie kissed her dad's cheek before he joined her mother on the front row. A radiant Maddie handed Angelina her bouquet before joining her hands with the groom's, and the ceremony began.

Grateful to still have the tissue in her hand, Angelina dabbed her eyes as the preacher talked about love and patience, and how they were the foundations of marriage. Throughout the service, Angelina couldn't help but think about her parents and how special their love story had been. The spell had brought them together, but it was their commitment and love for each other that had helped them endure the many storms life had thrown their way. In the end, their love hadn't been strong enough to beat cancer, but it *had* been strong enough to let them enjoy every single second they had together. They hadn't wasted their time on petty arguments or silly misunderstandings. They had been thankful for each and every day they could wake up together, until that very last morning when Samuel Clark had taken his last breath with his wife by his side.

By the time the minister pronounced Maddie and Nick man and wife, Angelina was a sobbing mess. The entire congregation was crying, too, so it was easy to brush off her tears as happy ones. And she *was* happy. Her best friend had found her happily ever after with the man of her dreams.

Angelina could feel the heat of someone's stare, and like a magnet, her gaze shifted to the second row.

While every head in the chapel was turned toward the happy couple, Dylan's eyes rested firmly on Angelina.

While the number of people invited to the wedding had been limited to close family and friends, the reception was open to anyone who had wanted to make the drive from Maple Ridge to the hotel in Gatlinburg. Because of the evening ceremony and the full-blown celebration expected to take place in the banquet hall, Angelina was grateful Felicia had recommended the guests stay overnight.

The party was in full swing, but Dylan was nowhere

to be found. Angelina had been busy, but now that her speech was over and her duties fulfilled, her eyes scanned the crowd in search of him. When the DJ announced it was time for the couple's first dance, Angelina took her second glass of champagne and retreated to a dark corner of the banquet hall.

As Maddie and Nick danced, Angelina couldn't help but smile as she watched the two of them. She couldn't help but think how wonderful it must be to have that kind of love—an honest, soul-stirring love—without the help of spells or charms or any other ridiculous magical enchantments.

Just two people, till death do them part.

The music changed, and more couples joined the bride and groom on the dance floor.

"Isn't there a rule that the maid of honor isn't supposed to be prettier than the bride?"

She smiled. His voice was soft and warm against her ear, and she trembled as his fingertips trailed across the exposed skin of her shoulder.

"The bride is the most beautiful woman in the room."

Dylan stepped closer, drawing her gently to his chest. She melted against him, loving the heat of his body as he held her close.

"I can't agree with you." He glided his nose along her skin, causing her to moan softly. "You're so gorgeous, Angelina. This dress is going to haunt my dreams for the rest of my life."

He gripped her waist and pulled them deeper into the corner. His lips ghosted over her, touching every inch of visible flesh his mouth could reach. Angelina's long black hair was swept up, granting him access to her shoulders and neck.

"You look so beautiful tonight," he murmured against her ear. "Seeing you walk down the aisle and listening to those vows . . . all I could think about was us."

"Us," Angelina said quietly, her voice quivering.

Burying his face against her neck, he sucked the skin there, and her head fell back against his shoulder.

"Look at them. Look at the way Nick's staring at her. As if he can't take a breath without her. I know how he feels, Angelina. I can't breathe without you."

Dylan gently bit her earlobe, making her groan.

"Just so there's no misunderstandings, I want this with you. All of this. The chapel. The rings. The vows. I want it all."

Her heartbeat accelerated as the enormity of his words washed over her.

"I want it, too," she admitted with a whisper.

Dylan smiled against her skin. His fingers danced along the straps of her halter dress, grateful to find that with one tug, the dress would easily fall away from her body.

"Do you know what else I want? I want you, Angelina. I love you, and I want you. Tonight."

Angelina whimpered as his teeth gently nipped at her neck.

"Not tonight. *Now*."

It was all he needed to hear. Dylan grabbed her hand, and without a backward glance at the partygoers, the two of them rushed toward the elevator.

The hotel room door had barely closed before he was

pushing her against it. Angelina grabbed his tie and pulled him closer, whimpering when their mouths collided.

"I love you," Dylan whispered in between kisses. "I love you so much."

Angelina closed her eyes, savoring his sweet words and heated touches as his hands skimmed the fabric of her dress. Her lips parted, and his tongue found hers, causing her to whimper louder and arch against him. Dylan groaned, grabbing her leg and hitching it around his waist as he pressed into her. Her hands wove into his hair as she kissed him harder.

"Please," she begged when they came up for air.

Breathing harshly, Dylan pressed his forehead against hers and gazed into her eyes. She was too beautiful . . . too eager . . . and he knew he had to slow down.

Dylan gently lowered her leg and took her by the hand, leading her toward the bed. Angelina gasped when she saw daisy petals scattered along the blanket.

"I know rose petals are typical," Dylan said sheepishly, "but nothing about us is typical."

"When did you—"

"That's why I was late to the reception," he said. "You wouldn't believe how hard it was to find daisies in this hotel."

Angelina's eyes welled. It was the most romantic thing she'd ever seen.

"They're beautiful. Thank you."

With trembling fingers, she reached for his tie. Dylan noticed her unease, and he took her hand, pulling it to his lips and kissing it softly.

"I'm nervous, too," he admitted.

"You are?"

"A little, yeah."

"But this isn't your first time."

"No, but it's yours, and I don't want you to regret a moment of it."

Feeling slightly braver, Angelina tugged the tie, letting it fall to the floor. She slipped her fingers beneath the buttons of his shirt, undoing each one with a slow, agonizing pace that made him tremble. He unzipped his slacks, letting them fall and pool at his feet. Angelina's appreciative gaze drifted over his body.

"Turn around, baby," he murmured, desperate to see her, too.

Angelina obeyed, and he let his hands slide along the straps of her dress. Her entire body shuddered when she felt his fingers undoing the tie. The dress fell away, leaving her in nothing but her lacy underwear and heels.

Angelina stepped out of her shoes and turned around.

His hungry gaze gave her courage, and she reached for her panties. The fabric drifted down her legs and joined her dress on the floor. Angelina loosened her hair, letting it spill around her shoulders, and Dylan's eyes drank her in, examining every curve.

Suddenly, he was the nervous one.

Hurting her was unimaginable.

"Hey," Angelina murmured as she took a step closer. "Don't worry. I'm not."

"You're not?"

She shook her head. "I'm nervous, but I'm not worried. Not about this. Do you know why?"

His hands settled on her hips as he drew her closer. "Why?"

"Do you remember asking me why I'd waited so

long?"

Dylan nodded.

"I've been waiting for you since I was thirteen years old. Ever since the day I cast that spell and blew out the candle. I wished for you, and now you're here. And you love me."

He pressed his forehead to hers. "I do. I love you so much."

Angelina placed her hands on each side of his face.

"I love you, too."

She'd never seen him smile so brightly.

"I do," she said, her eyes shining. "I love you."

With a groan that set her body on fire, Dylan lowered his mouth to hers. Angelina's fingers dug into his back, pulling him closer until the weight of his body pressed her down onto the mattress. Kissing hungrily, their fingers roamed along each other's skin. Dylan's hand cupped her breast, causing her to moan against his mouth as he teased and caressed her flesh. Lowering his head, he peppered kisses along the length of her body, making Angelina squirm beneath him as he blazed a trail between her breasts and down her stomach.

"Please," she whimpered.

Dylan's mouth never left her skin, even when he dipped his head lower, causing Angelina to moan as pleasure spiked through her body. Her fingers tangled in his hair as his fingers, and finally, his mouth slowly explored her. She arched, he groaned, and when she was sure she couldn't take another moment of his touch, her body shattered beneath him.

Overwhelmed and just a little giddy, Angelina began to giggle. He pressed a kiss to her inner thigh, and she felt him smile against her skin.

"That's been building for a while," Dylan said, smiling up at her.

"No kidding."

He chuckled before crawling off the bed. Angelina was about to protest, but then she realized what he was doing. Seconds later, she heard the rip of foil, and then he was back, hovering over her and kissing her tenderly.

"I love you," he whispered.

"I love you."

His eyes never left her face. Holding his breath, he watched Angelina's every grimace and felt every clutch of her fingers against his skin. He moved slowly, gently, until finally, the creases in her forehead started to fade, and her grasp on his shoulders began to relax.

Sex wasn't new territory for Dylan, but as he made love to the woman of his dreams, he couldn't help but think *this* should have been his first time, too. Every breathless whisper, every frantic touch, and every quiet breath vibrated through him, and when Angelina cried out his name, he felt a feral sense of pride, knowing he was the only man who would ever touch her this way, and his would be the only name she ever screamed.

Seventeen

Dylan was the first one to wake the next morning. His eyes hadn't even opened before he was pulling her closer, despite the fact they were already nestled in each other's arms. They'd fallen asleep just like this—with her back pressed to his chest and his arms draped around her. Burying his nose in her hair, he inhaled deeply, loving the scent of her. Of them.

He frowned as he felt his body respond to her closeness and warmth. Despite his intentions to be as tender as possible, he was sure she would need time to recuperate. They had made love twice last night. Hours had passed between each, and the second time had taken much longer than the first. Initially, Dylan had been too concerned with hurting her to really love her the way he'd wanted. The second time, however, Angelina had climbed on top of him, and he'd been more than willing to let her take control. They explored and discovered and even laughed, and when she finally fell asleep in his arms, he had stayed awake for hours, listening to her soft snores and loving the feel of her skin against his.

Angelina continued to sleep as he lowered the blanket, letting his fingertips drift along her spine. It was the one part of her body that had been kept hidden from him in the darkness, and he smiled as he explored the arch of her back. His eyes drifted lower, and that was when he saw her tattoo.

Dylan smiled, remembering the night when she'd refused to let him see it, and now he understood why. It was right on the curve of her hip, hidden discreetly each and every day. The design was a simple one of two small, intersecting hearts surrounded by vines. His fingers caressed the flesh as he wondered what it symbolized to her.

"You found my secret," Angelina said.

"Yes, I did." Dylan lowered his head, placing a gentle kiss along the ink. "Good morning, baby."

"Good morning."

He traced the outline of the hearts. "What does it mean?"

Angelina laughed quietly. "Maddie and I got matching tattoos when we turned eighteen. At the time, it represented us, but we also knew it could mean something more. Two intersecting hearts can signify friendship. Lovers. Husband and wife. Parent and child. The possibilities were endless, and that's why we chose it. We liked that it could symbolize so many different things. Our past. Our present. Our future."

Dylan crawled back up her body, wrapping his arms

around her and holding her close to his chest. Angelina turned her head in search of his lips, and she sighed softly when she found them.

"You're my future," he murmured. "You believe that, don't you?"

Angelina placed her palm against his cheek.

"I'm starting to, yeah."

They lay together, enjoying the quiet and warmth, until Angelina's rumbling stomach shattered the silence.

Dylan laughed. "Hungry?"

"Obviously." With a giggle, she turned around in his arms. "Checkout is at eleven. We should order room service and then get packed."

He nuzzled her nose. "I don't want to leave."

"Neither do I."

Dylan leaned in to kiss her just as his cell vibrated on the night stand.

"Not important," he murmured against her lips.

"It might be."

Sighing heavily, Dylan reached for his phone, not bothering to look down at the screen before barking hello at whoever dared to interrupt his perfect morning. He closed his eyes as David Murray's voice washed over him.

"Celia's in the hospital," David said.

Angelina managed to hold back her tears as Dr. Campbell explained that anemia wasn't unusual for chemotherapy patients, and this would explain why her mother had been suffering from fatigue and dizziness over the past few days.

Angelina and Dylan exchanged confused looks.

"We didn't know," Angelina murmured guiltily. "I

mean, she's been very nauseated, but she didn't tell us . . ."

"She told Mr. Murray," the doctor said. "That's why he brought her in. Celia wasn't a bit happy about it, either, but she didn't have the strength to fight him. It was a good thing he did, too. If she'd waited much longer, she might have required transfusions. As it is, we're going to prescribe some medication and monitor her closely until we get her hemoglobin levels closer to where they need to be. And we'll have to stop chemo for a while to give her body a chance to recover."

Angelina's head was swimming. *Now we're stopping chemo?*

"For how long?" Dylan asked.

"We're not sure yet. Let's see how she responds, okay?" Dr. Campbell placed a reassuring hand on Angelina's shoulder. "You can see her if you like."

Angelina nodded numbly, and Dylan took her hand, leading her down the hallway that led to Celia's room. Maybe it was the smell of antiseptic that seemed to permeate the hospital walls, but nausea hit her like a lightning bolt, and she gripped Dylan's arm for support.

"Are you okay?"

Angelina nodded as they continued down the hallway.

Her mom had been sicker than she'd let on, and it didn't take a genius to figure out why. Celia hadn't wanted anything to keep Angelina from attending the wedding.

"Here she is," Dylan said, pointing toward the room number. When they stepped inside, neither of them were surprised to find David sitting at Celia's side, holding her hand in his. He offered them a tired smile. Celia seemed to be resting. Her eyes were closed, and Angelina couldn't help but notice how pale her mother appeared.

Angelina wanted to cry. *Needed* to cry.

But she couldn't. She had to stay strong.

For now, anyway.

David gently placed Celia's hand on the bed before rising to his feet. Angelina walked straight to him, wrapping her arms around his neck and thanking him for taking such good care of her mom.

"She's very special to me," David whispered.

"I know she is."

David offered Angelina the chair next to her mom's bed, and she took it gratefully. Her head was still spinning, but at least the nausea was subsiding. She heard Dylan ask David if he'd like some coffee, and she was thankful. He knew she needed this time with her mom without an audience.

"Please don't go too far."

"We won't." Dylan leaned down and kissed her forehead before taking David's arm and leading him out into the hall.

Angelina's eyes raked over her mom's body. Reaching for Celia's hand, she noticed the coldness of her mother's skin and the faint blue shade of her fingernails. She knew enough about anemia to realize these were common symptoms, but that did little to relieve the knot of tension in Angelina's stomach.

Had her mom's nails been blue for days? How had she missed that?

"I wish there was some magic spell . . . some miraculous herb that could ease your pain. I wish my hands could do whatever they were designed to do. If there was something, you'd tell me, right? If there was some ancient spell that could make this go away, you'd tell me, wouldn't you?"

Angelina closed her eyes as the tears began to fall.

"I would," her mom's voice rasped, and Angelina's eyes snapped open. "If there was any way to ease your suffering, don't you think I would?"

"It's not my suffering I'm worried about."

Celia offered her daughter a weak smile.

"Why didn't you tell me how sick you were?" Angelina asked. "You needed me."

"Maddie needed you, and David took very good care of me. Besides, I knew this weekend would be important for you and Dylan, and I wouldn't have wanted you to miss a moment of it."

Despite her teary eyes, Angelina smiled.

"I told him I love him."

Celia's smile lit up her entire face.

"That's wonderful, Angelina. I believe he needed to hear that."

"I believe he did, too. I shouldn't have waited so long."

Celia squeezed her daughter's hand. It was just a gentle pressure, but it was comforting.

"And I shouldn't have hidden my symptoms from you. I'm sorry I did that, even if my intentions were good."

"Please don't do that again. I need to know everything. I can't take care of you if I don't."

"I won't," Celia promised.

Angelina spotted a bruise that had formed on her mother's arm, and she placed her finger along the purple blemish.

"It doesn't hurt," her mom said. "It's just part of it."

"I know. I could try to heal it."

Celia laughed softly. "Better not. The doctor might get suspicious if my bruises begin to fade too quickly."

Angelina grinned. She hadn't thought of that.

"Besides, healing isn't just done with the hands," Celia told her. "You can heal with your spirit. You can heal with your heart. That's what you do for me. Seeing you happy and in love with a wonderful man. Watching how devoted he is to you. And yes, we can give credit to the spell for bringing him into your life, but magic can only do so much. It's love, Angelina. It's love that keeps him here. Never doubt that."

Celia closed her eyes. Her breathing evened out and Angelina was sure she had drifted off to sleep, but suddenly, her mom's fragile voice filled the air once more.

"You heal me every day. You just can't see it. But trust me, you do."

"But will it be enough?"

Her mom's eyes drifted open, and she gave her daughter a watery smile.

"Yes, Angelina, I believe it will be enough."

Something passed between them—a brief moment of realization and understanding— and Angelina felt her spirits soar.

"There will be healing, Angelina—for all of us."

Celia's eyes closed, and her soft snores filled the air.

Overwhelmed with relief, Angelina buried her face in her hands and wept as her mom's words echoed in her ears.

There will be healing.

Dylan was surprised when Angelina asked him to take her home to Maple Ridge. Sure, Celia's hospital was just an hour away in Knoxville, but he'd expected Angelina to demand a cot. The doctor had explained that Celia would most likely sleep the rest of the night, and Mr. Murray had offered to stay at the hospital, giving Angelina and Dylan the chance to go home if they wished.

When he and David had returned to the room, Angelina was weeping while Celia slept peacefully. Dylan had no idea what had transpired in the fifteen minutes they'd stepped out to get coffee, but whatever it was had convinced Angelina it was okay to return home for the night. She was smiling a little too brightly despite her tears, but he would never complain about her smiles, especially after the day she had endured.

When it was time for bed, it wasn't even a question if he would stay.

After stripping down to nothing, Angelina and Dylan crawled into bed, wrapping the blanket around them. Once again, she took the lead, straddling his hips and hovering above him. Dylan moaned as she settled herself on him, and she laced her fingers through his hands as they began to move. He closed his eyes, letting her control their every movement, until finally he had to touch her, too. Letting go of her hands, he gripped her hips and raised himself up, causing Angelina to whimper when his mouth molded to hers.

Home sweet home.

When Celia was released from the hospital three days later, Dylan noticed a distinct change in Angelina's mood. She smiled all the time—even when she was administering her mom's medicine or begging Celia to take "just one more bite." Peace resonated around the two of them, and while he was thrilled, Dylan couldn't help but wish they would share a small part of that tranquility with him when it came to dealing with his father.

He still had no idea what to do about his dad's job offer.

Dylan had to admit his old man was persistent. Charles or Beth emailed daily, asking if he needed more information, more money, more perks. Dylan wasn't crazy. He knew the other columnists weren't given the same royal treatment, and he hated that the nepotism had started already. Regardless, he couldn't deny the money was fantastic, and he would be a fool to turn it down.

But could he really work for a man he despised?

Dylan was still contemplating that question when he arrived at Angelina's shop later in the afternoon. He was stunned to find her sitting on the counter, clutching a piece of paper in her hand.

"Baby?"

Angelina's head snapped up. Her eyes were red-rimmed, and the image nearly tore his heart in two.

Slowly, he walked toward the counter, stepping between her legs. Angelina sighed as his hands soothingly rubbed her arms.

"Baby, what's wrong?"

Angelina wiped her eyes. "When my dad died, we placed the money from his life insurance policy into a savings account. It wasn't a lot, but it had been enough to take care of mom's treatments and medication. But we weren't prepared for so many rounds of chemo, and we didn't expect the stronger, more expensive medicine this time around. And . . ."

Her voice trailed off, and Dylan took the paper out of

her hand.

It was her monthly bank statement.

And the balance was less than a thousand dollars.

Dylan had picked up enough of Celia's prescriptions to know how costly they were. He had never asked about her treatments, but he knew they were expensive.

"What about Social Security?" He had no idea how that worked.

"Mom isn't nearly old enough."

"Any other insurance?"

Angelina shook her head. "She's never had any."

"And it would be impossible to get it now."

Angelina nodded. "I've sat here all afternoon, wondering how I'm going to explain to my sick mom that the money is just . . . gone. We have income from the shop, but that's how we take care of all the other bills."

She sniffled quietly and glanced around her father's store.

"I love this place so much. It's been in my family since I was a little girl. Mom's dream was to have a shop just like this, and because my dad lived to make her every dream come true, he bought it for her. But . . . I don't know. I've had some offers for it over the years. Maybe it's time."

"No, Angelina." He brushed a strand of hair away from her face. "Don't sell your shop. We'll figure something out."

Angelina smiled gently. "It's not your problem, Dylan."

"It is my problem. It's *our* problem. And we'll work it out." He pulled her into his arms, resting his forehead against hers as quiet tears spilled down her cheeks. "Please don't cry. I promise we'll figure it out."

The answer was ridiculously easy.

Dylan may have despised his father, but he loved Angelina, and there wasn't anything he wouldn't do to dry her tears.

Eighteen

"It's good to see you, Dylan."

"I appreciate you taking the time to speak with me."

Charles offered his son a chair before returning to his desk. "I'm very happy to hear you're considering my offer."

"I'm willing to listen to what you have to say, yes."

"I'm glad. May I ask what changed your mind?"

Dylan had been expecting this question.

"I want to live close to Maple Ridge, and this job would allow me to do that. Your offer is unbelievably generous, and I'd be crazy not to consider it. But mostly, I'm here because I am in love with a beautiful, kind-hearted woman who has taught me that family is everything, and she believes I'll regret it for the rest of my life if I don't have at least one civil conversation with my father."

Charles smiled.

"Well, why don't we talk business first, and then we'll work on the civil conversation."

Dylan nodded.

"It's a weekly column," Charles explained, handing him a detailed sheet, listing the job description and ridiculous pay, along with a nice bonus to help with moving expenses. Dylan was sure none of the other columnists had such perks, but he wasn't about to argue. Not anymore.

"Your deadline is Wednesday at noon, and your article would run in Friday's edition. Like I said, we're looking for human interest stories. Hometown heroes, thriving local businesses . . . things of that sort. A local soldier is returning home after a two-year stint in Afghanistan. He's agreed to an interview, and we'd like that to be your first feature."

"And Beth would remain my editor?"

"Yes, you will continue to report to Beth. Your interaction with me would be minimal."

It was music to Dylan's ears, and he was tempted to sign on the spot.

"It's an amazing opportunity, and I appreciate the offer. When would you need my decision?"

"Well, I was hoping you'd decide today. If it's such an amazing opportunity, why wait?"

"Because I'd like to discuss it with Angelina."

Charles leaned back in his chair and appraised his son. "I assume Angelina is the beautiful, kind-hearted woman?"

"That's right."

"And you need her permission to accept a job offer?"

Dylan took a deep breath. *Try to keep your temper under control.*

"It's not about permission. When you love someone, you should make important decisions together."

Charles smiled ruefully. "That's good advice. Maybe that's why I've been married—and divorced—three times."

Maybe so.

"Still, you're awfully young to be so serious about one woman, aren't you? I'd hate to see you lose focus of your career—"

"Trust me. My focus is exactly where it should be."

An awkward silence filled the air until Charles finally cleared his throat.

"We'd like to hire someone within the next two weeks."

"No problem. I'll contact you as soon as possible."

With business out of the way, Dylan knew he had two choices. He could walk right out the door, or he could attempt to have a conversation with his father. He could ask the questions that had haunted him for years, and maybe—just maybe—his dad would answer them.

"Why did you leave?"

Charles's eyes widened. "You cut right to the chase, don't you?"

"When I want answers, yes."

"That's what makes you a good reporter. Just like your old man," his father said, his eyes twinkling with pride.

"That's where our similarities end."

Dylan watched as his dad's face flashed with sadness and regret.

"I wasn't a good husband, Dylan. I worked too many long hours and neglected your mother for years. When she told me she was pregnant, I honestly didn't believe you were mine because I couldn't remember the last time we'd had sex. *That's* how neglectful I was."

Rising from his chair, Charles walked toward the window and adjusted the blinds before gazing out into the sunshine.

"Writing was all I wanted to do. Freelance is a great place to start in this business—if you're single and don't mind starving to death. But when you have a wife and child depending on you, writing for pennies isn't the most financially viable option. Along with writing, I worked second and third jobs, and I was grateful to have a place to go because home was a war zone. Your mother and I argued constantly. Patti wanted me to find a stable job. She wanted me home more. She wanted a marriage. She wanted me to be a father to you. But I was young and selfish. Nothing was more important to me than becoming a writer."

"Not even your wife?"

"Not even my wife. Not even my son."

Anger churned in Dylan's stomach.

"When she asked for a divorce, I felt as if a weight had been lifted from my shoulders. I know that must sound horrible, coming from your father, but it's the truth. I wasn't a good husband. I was a worse father. But I *was* a great writer. I justified it in my head, telling myself that when I became successful, I'd go back and be the father you needed me to be. But it took nearly a decade to establish myself in publishing. By that time you were a teenager, and I knew you hated me. Why wouldn't you?

Through friends, I'd kept tabs on your mother, and I knew she was now a college professor. You were both doing just fine without me. Staying away was the very best thing I could do for you."

Dylan scrutinized his father as he returned to his chair. His dad had become a successful newspaper publisher while he and his mom had struggled to make ends meet for years. Charles Thomas was, without a doubt, the most selfish person Dylan had ever met. Bile rose in this throat as he considered actually working for the man, and if Dylan had been a single man, he would have told his father to kiss his ass.

But he wasn't a single man—not in his heart, anyway.

"Why are you reaching out to me now?"

"I read one of your articles in the magazine. I thought the name was just a coincidence, but I did some digging and found out that you were, indeed, my son. I've . . . sort of followed your career ever since. I was finally in a position to help you, so I called your mother. She told me to go to hell."

Dylan smiled proudly.

"But I'm a persistent bastard, and I kept calling. All I wanted was the chance to talk to you and maybe help with your career, if you'd let me."

"She told me you'd called."

"I know. When I called back, she admitted you'd lost your job and your heart was set on working in this area. That's when I had Beth offer you the freelance position. It would get you established with our newspaper, at least, until something better opened up. When our Friday columnist decided to retire, I knew it was the perfect opportunity for you. Yes, you're my son, and yes, I'm trying to make amends, but I wouldn't offer you this job if I didn't think you were qualified for it. My newspaper's reputation is far too important to me."

"Shrewd boss. Shitty father."

Charles wasn't offended in the least. "I can't argue with either of those points. But I'd like the chance to be a better father, if you'd let me."

Dylan's first inclination was to tell him that he'd done just fine without a father for twenty years and he didn't need one now. But then he thought of Angelina and how she'd give anything to spend just one more day with her dad.

"I'm going to need to think about that."

Charles nodded. "I understand."

Dylan rose to his feet, and his father followed him to the door.

"I'll let you know about the job as soon as possible. Thank you for the opportunity."

Determined to be polite, Dylan extended his hand.

"My pleasure," Charles said, gripping his son's hand. "And thank *you* . . . for the opportunity."

"It was good to see Celia eat tonight."

Angelina and Dylan were snuggled under her blanket in her bed. It was after midnight, and her mom was sleeping peacefully down the hall.

"It was," she agreed, nuzzling his chest. "Her appetite is slowly coming back."

Dylan slid his fingers along her spine. "Is your mom a light sleeper?"

"Not usually, why?"

His fingers drifted lower, causing Angelina to

tremble. "I missed you today, baby."

"I missed you, too, but we are not having sex in my mother's house."

"Never?"

"Not while she's home, no."

He pretended to pout, and Angelina laughed, kissing him gently.

"Besides, you're stalling. I want to hear about your conversation with your father."

Dylan sighed and stared up at the ceiling.

"It's a good offer, and I think I'm going to accept it, even if the sight of the man makes me sick. I won't have to report to him, so that's a plus."

"If you hate him so much, maybe working for him isn't the best idea. There are other jobs."

"Not with these benefits."

Dylan told her about the outrageous salary and bonuses, and her eyes widened.

"Wow. Maybe I should write for a living."

Dylan shook his head. "That's not typical for a newspaper columnist. Trust me. Nepotism and paternal guilt are definitely at work here."

"Well, I'm proud of you for even talking to him and keeping your temper in check. I know that must have been hard."

"You're just glad you didn't get a call from the Knoxville PD."

"I *am* glad. I was kind of expecting one."

They both laughed.

"Can I ask a question?" she asked, and he nodded. "If you hate him so much, and if you know the offer is ridiculous, why are you considering it?"

His arms tightened around her.

"Let me just say upfront this is a fight you won't win."

Angelina's eyes narrowed. "Why would we fight?"

"Because you're stubborn and proud and . . ."

He continued to babble, and it didn't take her long to figure it out. Angelina raised herself up on her elbow and gave him an annoyed glare.

"Dylan Thomas, you'd better not be taking this job for me."

"I'm taking this job for *us*. I'm taking this job because it really is the perfect scenario. I can work in Knoxville and live in Maple Ridge. I can be with you, which is what I want. I'm serious when I say I love you and that I want to marry you. And I know you aren't ready to discuss it, but you need to know that's how I feel. I'm never going to want anyone else, and it's time you accepted it. I want to build a life with you. Building a life takes a steady income, and this job offers that."

Her eyes softened. "And all of that is wonderful, and I want it, too, but that's not the only reason you're taking this job."

Dylan sighed and pulled her close, pressing his lips against her cheek.

"No, it's not the only reason. I'm taking this job because the salary is insane. There's even a moving bonus. From the day I sign my contract, I can help you with Celia's medical bills, and you'll never have to sell your shop."

Angelina tried to keep her tears at bay.

"But . . . you hate your dad."

"And that may never change. I've always heard love is

202

stronger than hate, and I never really understood what that meant, but I do now. I love you more than I could ever hate him, and that's why I'm accepting his job offer."

Through her tears, Angelina gazed into his eyes, and she was overwhelmed by the emotion she saw reflected in them.

In that moment, everything was crystal clear.

Magic was an amazing force that could forever change your life.

It could hurt.

It could heal.

There will be healing.

"You really love me."

Dylan smiled and stroked her cheek. "Are you just now realizing that?"

It wasn't as if she had ever doubted his words. She'd just refused to truly embrace them, fearing that his every thought and emotion was being manipulated by the spell. But to accept a job he really didn't want, just to take care of her family and to build a life together . . .

Tonight, she finally believed him.

"I love you, too," Angelina said softly.

Later, after Dylan had fallen asleep, Angelina crept out of bed and carefully opened her bedroom door. She walked down the hallway and headed straight to her mom's room.

She wasn't surprised to find Celia sitting up against the headboard. Angelina smiled and pulled a seat closer to her mom's bedside. Mother and daughter linked hands, and Angelina noticed that hers weren't the only pair of blue eyes filled with tears.

"You understand now, don't you?"

Angelina nodded. "The spell brought us together, but love keeps him here."

Celia smiled. "That's right."

"You knew all along, didn't you?"

Her mother didn't bother denying it.

"There will be a reunion between father and son," Celia whispered, giving her daughter's hand a squeeze. "There will be a beautiful wedding at the pond, and there will be a granddaughter with lovely blue eyes who will blow out her own candle when she turns thirteen."

Angelina smiled brightly. "And what about you?"

"Don't worry about me," Celia murmured. "I won't miss a single second of any of it."

Nineteen

Angelina didn't know when it happened, but as she gazed across the pond, she couldn't deny the evidence.

Fall had arrived in Maple Ridge.

The mountains were blanketed in shades of crimson and gold. It was her favorite time of year, because there were few things more beautiful than a Smoky Mountain autumn.

It had been nearly two months since Maddie's wedding. She and Nick were happy and content in their little house in Atlanta, and Angelina had already made plans to visit them later in the fall.

Celia's weekly chemo treatments had resumed. The nausea was still crippling at times, and her hair was nearly gone. Thanks to sweet neighbors and friends, Celia now had an assorted collection of colorful scarves and pretty hats. David Murray was always by her side, and Angelina couldn't help but be grateful that her mom had such a supportive and devoted companion.

In two weeks, they would find out if the chemo was doing its job.

Dylan had started working at his father's newspaper. His relationship with his dad was still strained, but Charles had kept his promise, and he'd had very little interaction with his son. Dylan enjoyed writing, and his article about the soldier returning home from Afghanistan had made the front page.

As for Angelina, the shop was busier than ever. She had hired Kelsey, a local singer who was studying music education at UT, to work part-time at the store. Angelina knew she would eventually need to find a new business partner, but for now, she and Kelsey were handling things just fine.

True to his word—and despite her arguments— Dylan had deposited his signing bonus into her savings account. The amount was obscene, but it was more than enough to cover Celia's medical expenses for the time being. Angelina worried about the future, but Dylan promised they would deal with whatever, whenever it came.

Which was good, because his mother was coming to Maple Ridge.

Today.

Angelina had been thrilled when Dylan had mentioned that his mom was eager to meet her. Her momentary excitement had swiftly turned to panic when she realized he meant *this* weekend. She had never officially met a boyfriend's mother, and Angelina couldn't shake the feeling that she wasn't prepared at all.

Sighing deeply, Angelina pulled her knees close to her

chest and closed her eyes as the soft autumn breeze wafted across her face. It was always chillier next to the water, but the fall temperatures made it even colder.

"Should have brought a sweater," she muttered.

As soon as the words escaped her lips, she felt the warmth of his body as he settled behind her. Angelina smiled as a pair of strong arms wrapped around her, pulling her close to his chest.

"You're early," Angelina said quietly. "Is she here?"

"Yeah, she's up at the house with your mom. They're already best friends."

Angelina laughed.

"We'll give them a few minutes," he said, kissing the side of her neck. "Are you cold, baby?"

"A little."

He snuggled her close.

"It's so pretty out here in the fall. I knew it would be."

Angelina grinned. "You don't have trees in Nashville?"

"Not like these."

She sighed and leaned her head back against his shoulder. "What if she hates me?"

"You can't seriously be worried about that."

Angelina shrugged.

"Baby, she will love you. Not as much as I do, but it'll be close."

"Does she know . . . everything?"

"She knows you waved your magic wand and put a spell on me, yes."

"I don't have a wand," Angelina grumbled.

Dylan chuckled. "It doesn't matter what she thinks. It

doesn't matter how she feels. I love you. I want to marry you. I want you to have my babies, and I pray they have your pretty blue eyes and my charming personality."

It wasn't the first time he'd said he wanted to marry her, but it *was* the first time he had mentioned kids.

Should she tell him about the blue-eyed daughter her mom had already prophesied?

Probably not.

Instead, she twisted around, wrapping her arms around his neck.

"That's what I want, too."

A slow grin crept across his face. "You do?"

"I do."

Something flashed in his eyes, and Angelina could feel the excitement radiating from him as he pulled her face close to his.

"Marry me."

Angelina giggled. "You're so impatient."

He grinned and kissed her softly.

"Now marry me."

She smiled. "I think I need to meet your mom first, don't you?"

Dylan sighed and pressed his forehead to hers.

"Soon. Promise me."

Angelina gently placed her hand against his cheek.

"Soon, I promise."

Any nervousness that Angelina felt about meeting Patti Thomas completely vanished when she and Dylan walked into the living room. She was sitting next to Celia, and when Patti's eyes settled on Angelina, she immediately leapt from the couch and wrapped the young woman in her arms.

"It's so nice to meet you, Angelina."

"It's nice to meet you, too."

Patti pulled Angelina by the hand and led her to the couch. Dylan took a seat in the corner and watched the three most important women in his life talk as if they had been friends forever. At one point, Angelina's eyes found his, and he winked—his silent way of saying *I told you so*. Angelina just smiled at him before resuming her conversation with his mother.

After a while, Dylan offered to make dinner for everyone. He was getting pretty good at spaghetti and meatballs, and it was the one food that, unbelievably, Celia was able to keep down. He was just starting the sauce when she walked into the room.

"Afraid I'll burn down your kitchen?" Dylan teased.

Celia laughed and sat down at the table. "I just wanted to give the two of them the chance to get to know each other. Besides, you and I need to have a talk of our own."

Dylan grinned and put the sauce on to simmer before joining Celia at the table. She reached for his hand, and he was happy to feel the warmth of her skin. She'd been cold and pale for so long.

"I haven't had the chance to thank you."

He'd been expecting this. What he hadn't expected was the emotion in her soft voice.

"You don't have to thank me, Celia."

"That's not true. Random acts of selfless love aren't common in this world. When you're the recipient of such a gift, you should thank the giver. You have taken a burden off my daughter's shoulders—a burden that shouldn't be hers—and I can't tell you how much I appreciate it. There's no way I could ever repay you."

"There's nothing to repay," he murmured, squeezing her hand. "I love your daughter, and I love you. Some guys aren't lucky enough to have even *one* great mom. I have two."

Celia's eyes glistened with tears.

"I don't know what the future holds with me and my dad," Dylan said, "but in the grand scheme of things, it really doesn't matter. I have my family. I have my mother, you, and Angelina. And hopefully, our family will grow."

"Oh, it will grow."

Excited to hear this amazing piece of news, Dylan scooted his seat a little closer. His voice was just a whisper. "Little girls with pretty blue eyes? Please say yes."

Celia grinned. "You are so impatient."

"Your daughter just told me the same thing," he said with a smirk. "Come on. I *know* you know something."

Her eyes sparkled. "What do you think? I have a crystal ball or something?"

"No way. You have *spiritual dreams*."

The two of them laughed, and Celia patted his hand.

"I think you're going to be very happy," she said.

Dylan smiled triumphantly. It was all the confirmation he needed.

After dinner, Dylan and Celia took the dog for a walk around the pond, leaving Patti and Angelina in the living room, looking over some of her family's photo albums.

"This is fascinating," Patti said, gliding her fingers along the picture in the album. "You have your grandmother's eyes."

"All of the girls in our family have blue eyes," Angelina explained. "It's the one family trait that doesn't seem to skip a generation."

As they flipped through the pages of the family album, Patti asked questions about everything from Abigail's boozing husband to mountain cures for eczema. When Angelina explained that she didn't really practice magic, Patti seemed disappointed.

"But that's such a gift. Why wouldn't you?"

"After my father's death, I was so conflicted and bitter. I have the gift to heal, but I couldn't heal him. So I . . . rebelled, I guess."

"And you can't heal your mom, so it's kind of like having this fantastic gift that renders you useless."

"Exactly," Angelina whispered, gently closing the photo album.

Patti smiled. "But you *aren't* useless. You know that right? You are a lovely, twenty-one-year-old woman who owns a successful company. You are a dream daughter, and you have captured the heart of my son. In my eyes, that makes you pretty perfect."

Angelina felt her blush creep across her cheek. "I'm far from perfect."

"And you're far from useless. You have other gifts. Reliable gifts. You have burdens and worries with which a young woman should never be faced. But despite everything, you have a kind heart and a strong spirit. You should be so proud of that."

"I don't always feel strong."

"Oh, I understand that, too. I raised a little boy all by myself. There were many days I just wanted to throw the blanket over my head and weep. But I couldn't. I had this adorable, brown-eyed toddler, and I was literally all he had in the whole world."

Angelina grinned, imagining Dylan as a little boy.

"I've never seen him in love," Patti said quietly. "It's remarkable, really. He's always been pretty quick-tempered and impatient, but with you he's very, very different."

Angelina didn't tell her he still had a problem with his temper and patience. Instead, she asked the one question that weighed heavily on her mind.

"And you aren't upset about the spell?"

Patti laughed. "When he first told me about that, I can't deny I was a little skeptical. But after meeting you and seeing the two of you together, I think it's obvious that *something* brought you together. You even convinced him to speak to his father."

Angelina sighed. "I hope it's a good thing."

"I think it could be. I would never tell Dylan this, but he reminds me very much of his father back when we were young. Charles was handsome, charming, and talented. He was also very determined to become a professional writer. Having a family wasn't in his plans, but it happened, and we were happy for a while. He wasn't a bad man, but he was neglectful, and my son deserved better. When I remember the nights my three-year-old cried himself to sleep because all he wanted was to see his dad . . ." Patti's voice trailed off, and she shook her head. "Anyway, it was a long time ago, and Dylan was a dream kid. His grades weren't the best, but that's just because he was stubborn and didn't care about anything but basketball and writing. He didn't really rebel until he was in college and joined that punk rock band. Has he shown you his god-awful tattoo?"

Angelina giggled, not daring to mention that she had one of her own. "Yes, I've seen it."

"I can tell by the expression on your face that you love it."

She grinned. "I do."

Patti sighed dramatically, and the two of them dissolved into laughter.

Cash's noisy bark echoed from the porch, and moments later, Dylan and Celia walked back into the living room. Angelina couldn't help but notice how tired her mom appeared, and she jumped to her feet.

"I'm fine," her mom assured her.

"We overdid it, I think." Dylan closed the door behind him. He couldn't hide the concern in his eyes as he watched Celia closely.

"I'm just a little tired." Celia smiled apologetically at their guest. "I'm stubborn. I try to do more than I should."

"I'd be the same way, so I completely understand," Patti said. She stood up and grabbed her bag. "It's getting late, anyway. I should head back to the hotel."

They said their goodbyes, and Patti promised to come back for breakfast in the morning before Angelina took her mom by the hand and led her down the hallway. Dylan watched them go, and he felt a tightening in his chest when he heard the soft click of Celia's bedroom door.

What if she's really sick? What if Angelina needs me?

"You should stay. I can find my way back to town."

Dylan turned to find his mother smiling softly in his direction.

"No, it'll be okay. She'll . . . she'll call if she needs me."

Patti walked toward her son and placed her hand

against his cheek.

"Your heart is here," she said simply.

He couldn't deny it.

"Definitely spellbound," Patti murmured.

He couldn't deny that either, although it wasn't entirely accurate.

"Mom, it's not just magic."

"I know, sweetheart. And that's why you should stay. I'll see you at breakfast."

They shared a hug before Dylan led his mom to the porch. After saying goodnight, he watched until she was safely in her car before stepping back inside, locking the door behind him.

After checking Cash's bowl, he turned off all the lights before making his way toward Celia's room. The door was open, and he peeked inside. Celia was resting peacefully in her bed, and Angelina was right by her side, watching her mom drift off to sleep. The expression on her face was soft and sad, but there were no tears.

No tears is always a good sign.

Sensing his eyes on her, Angelina turned her head toward the door. They smiled at one another before she stood up from her chair and quietly walked out into the hallway.

"She's okay?" Dylan asked.

"Yeah, I think the busy day just caught up with her."

Dylan nodded.

"I thought you were going back to the hotel with your mom?"

"I didn't want to leave you."

"I didn't want you to leave."

She took him by the hand and led him down the

hallway to her bedroom. When they were both inside, Angelina quietly closed the door. She twisted the lock and turned around. Dylan stepped closer, gently pinning her against the door. Her breath quickened when he dipped his head, letting his lips brush against her throat.

"Angelina, I never want to leave."

Her fingers twined in his hair. "Good. That saves me from having to beg you to stay."

He trailed his lips along her jaw and up along her ear, causing her to tremble.

"I love you," he said.

Moaning softly, Angelina pulled his face close to hers. His eyes were desperate and needy, but it wasn't just desire she saw reflecting in his brown eyes. He loved her. He had proven it time and time again, and it was time for her to do the same.

Soon, she promised herself.

They slowly undressed each other, and Angelina led him over to her bed. They fell onto the mattress, tangled in each other's arms and kissing hungrily. Dylan hovered above her, and his smile was triumphant as she wrapped her legs around his waist.

"I thought we weren't having sex in your mother's house?"

Angelina grinned and tightened her legs around him.

"Maybe just this once," she whispered.

Twenty

Dr. Campbell's office was as cold and sterile as ever. Angelina closed her eyes, praying this would be the last time she ever had to sit in this chair.

Celia had finished her latest round of chemo, and the scans were now complete. Today, they would find out if the treatments had been successful. Despite Celia's assurance that she was going to be just fine, Angelina couldn't seem to stop shaking.

Dylan clutched her left hand. Her mom was sitting to her right. As always, Celia was the calm one. Angelina wished she had the same faith in magic her mother possessed.

After today, maybe she would.

Maybe . . .

The door clicked, and Angelina's heart leapt into her throat as Dr. Campbell walked in, greeting them warmly before leaning on the edge of his desk.

"Please have good news," Angelina whispered.

Dr. Campbell smiled softly at her.

"I have wonderful news. Your mother's scans are clear."

The scans are clear.

Tears trickled down Angelina's face as the doctor explained that he would like to schedule follow-up visits every three months. She tried to listen, but all she could focus on were those four little words.

The scans are clear.

No more treatments. No more surgery.

She tilted her head toward her mom. Celia was smiling and listening carefully to the doctor's instructions. Angelina then turned toward Dylan, and his eyes were on her. His relieved smile was stretched across his face.

Angelina squeezed his hand, and in that moment—as she watched Dylan wipe away his own tears—she felt her entire life shift into its proper place. For so long, she had rebelled against her heritage. She'd fought against her natural gifts and had grown bitter and pessimistic about life and love.

No more.

Life was too short, too unpredictable, and too uncertain to deny herself any semblance of happiness.

And that happiness was starting tonight.

After a celebratory dinner of spaghetti and meatballs, Angelina led Dylan down to the pond.

"When's your birthday?" Angelina asked as they spread a blanket on the ground. Dylan had another one tucked beneath his arm, and he wrapped it around the two of them as they settled onto the grass. Angelina sat between his legs, and he enveloped her in his arms.

"It's in December. Why?"

"I'm going to buy you a cookbook."

Dylan chuckled and kissed the side of her neck. "Tired of my cooking? Your mom loves my spaghetti."

She grinned. "I know."

They snuggled close and gazed across the water. After a while, Angelina pointed toward the grassy field just beyond the pond.

"Did you know that's mine?"

"The land?"

Angelina nodded. "It was a gift from my parents before dad passed away. He said I might want my own place someday."

"It would be a pretty spot for a house."

"I think so, too."

"And it'd be close to your mom."

Angelina grinned. He knew how important that would be to her.

She twisted around in his arms.

"Dylan, will you build me a house?"

"I'll build you anything you want."

"Will you cook something besides spaghetti in our pretty kitchen?"

"I'll take a gourmet cooking class if it will make you happy."

"Will you marry me?"

"I'll . . ." he blinked rapidly. "Wait . . . what did you say?"

Angelina gently traced his bottom lip with her finger.

"Will you marry me?"

He inhaled sharply.

"Are you proposing to me?"

Angelina nodded. "I was reminded today that life is too short. People say it all the time, but I don't think they realize how true it is. Cancer is scary. *Life* is scary. I could die tomorrow. So if I can be happy *today*, why wouldn't I choose to be? I've spent so much time worrying about everything. My dad. My mom. The shop. The spell. Mom once told me that I've fought so hard against what I'm destined to be that I've forgotten who I am, and she's right."

Dylan stroked her cheek. "So, who are you?"

Smiling, Angelina playfully pushed him back against the blanket. She crawled over him, and his hands settled against her hips as they stared into each other's eyes.

"I'm a mountain witch, and when I was thirteen years old, I cast a spell and wished for you."

Dylan grinned. "And now I'm here."

"And now you're here."

"What are you going to do with me?"

Angelina teased his mouth with hers. "I'm going to marry you—right here at this pond. And we're going to build a house and have a beautiful, blue-eyed daughter."

"Just one?"

"Mom's only seen one so far."

Dylan smiled and rolled them over so that he could gaze down into her sweet eyes.

"This wasn't a very traditional proposal, Angelina."

"Nothing about us has been traditional."

"I know, but this should be the one thing we do like normal people. I should be on my knee. Or at least have a ring."

"Do you want me to take it back?"

Dylan frowned. "You can't just take back a proposal. You don't ask someone to build you a house and be your husband and then just take it back."

"You forgot the gourmet cooking class."

Her giggle was silenced with his passionate kiss, and when he finally lifted his eyes to hers once again, they were both breathless.

"Will you marry me, right here at this pond?" Dylan murmured.

It wasn't the fairy tale proposal she'd envisioned as a little girl.

It was better.

"Yes," she replied softly.

The next day, Dylan was sitting behind his desk at the office, finishing up his article on this weekend's harvest festival in the Smokies. The other columnists couldn't help but notice that he was in an unusually good mood, and it didn't even cross his mind to keep the news a secret. He'd said *I'm getting married* more times than he could count, and he loved the way the three little words just rolled off his tongue.

They'd rolled off his tongue many times since last night.

Naturally, Celia was the first to know, and while she promised that she hadn't predicted the exact timing, she'd had a "feeling" it would be her daughter doing the proposing. Dylan still wasn't sure how he felt about that, but in the grand scheme of things, he knew it didn't truly matter.

All that mattered was Angelina had said yes.

The first calls had been to his mom and Maddie. Both

had been ecstatic, and Maddie's high-pitched scream still resonated in his ears.

There was only one person left to tell, and while Dylan wasn't sure it was necessary, Angelina seemed to think otherwise.

So far, Dylan's interaction with his father had been limited. He hadn't even stepped inside the boss's office since the day he'd accepted the job. Charles didn't usually deal with the writers—he left that to the lead editors in each department—so there had been no risk of accidentally bumping into each other at the copy machine.

I'll just tell him I'm getting married and then walk out, Dylan told himself as he rode the elevator to the sixth floor. The doors opened, and he nodded to the receptionist who told him he could go right in. He knocked anyway, and he waited to hear his dad's voice before heading inside.

"Well, this is a surprise," Charles said, folding the latest edition of the paper and placing it on his desk. "To what do I owe the honor?"

Dylan closed the door, and his dad offered him a seat.

"I don't know why I'm telling you this—or if you even care to know—but I'm getting married."

Charles's face flashed with surprise.

"Mom and Angelina both thought you should know, so I'm telling you. We haven't set a date, but it will be as soon as possible." Dylan took a deep breath. "I'm not here for fatherly advice, so don't strain yourself by trying to come up with something. They just thought you should know your only son is getting married."

"And what about you? Don't you think I should know?"

"I don't think you care one way or another."

Charles sighed. "You'd be wrong about that, and I wouldn't insult you by offering any fatherly advice. I doubt there's a thing I can teach you about being a good husband."

Dylan didn't know what to say to that, and anything he did say would probably sound like an insult, so he decided to keep his mouth shut.

"Congratulations, son."

"Thank you."

"I assume you'll be living in Maple Ridge?"

Dylan nodded. "We're going to build a house close to her mom's."

"I know some local contractors. I could give you some names."

"You don't have to do that."

"I'd like to," Charles said. "What good is having a dad with connections if you don't use them from time to time?"

Dylan honestly didn't have a clue about hiring a reputable contractor, so he agreed to let his father give him some recommendations.

"I'm assuming you're getting married before the house is finished?"

"Yeah, I'm pretty impatient." Dylan grinned, and his dad smiled in return. "We'll live with her mom until it's ready. I practically live there anyway."

"Sounds like you have everything under control."

Dylan frowned. "Yeah, I just need to find a jewelry store."

"You need a ring?" Charles asked. "I have a friend who owns a jewelry store downtown. We could go take a look if you like."

"You have a lot of friends."

Charles laughed. "That tends to happen when you're the owner of a metro newspaper. Spencer's Jewelry is a good choice. It's a family-owned store that's been in business for over fifty years. The manager's name is Kirk. He'll take good care of you."

"I appreciate that."

Charles jotted down the address and handed it to his son.

"Damn, your handwriting is as bad as mine."

His dad laughed. "Don't worry. I think our penmanship is the only thing we have in common. Well, that and our brown eyes."

With a sigh, Dylan glanced down at his watch. This could be the biggest mistake of his life, but he was happy today, so he decided to give it a shot.

"It's nearly lunch time," Dylan said. "Would you . . . want to grab something to eat? And then maybe we could hit that jewelry store. I've never picked out a ring before, and since you know the guy . . ."

Charles couldn't hide his smile.

"Yeah, that sounds good. Just let me make a call?"

Dylan nodded and tried to control his bouncing leg.

"Krista," his dad said into the phone, "would you please clear my schedule for the afternoon? I'm taking my son to lunch."

"Well, you're right. This burger's delicious."

Charles squirted ketchup onto his plate. "I told you this place is great. It's one of the few family-operated restaurants left on this block. Been around for decades."

"You seem to be very into family businesses."

"I'm into helping the local economy and small-business owners. The economy is horrible and families are struggling. I like to help if I can."

"Yeah, taking care of family is important."

An awkward silence filled the air as the men continued to eat.

"So, tell me about this fiancée of yours."

Dylan smiled. *Fiancée.*

"She must really be something if that grin on your face is any indication," Charles said, chuckling.

"She's amazing, yeah."

As they ate, Dylan talked about the news story that brought him to Maple Ridge. Charles nearly fell out of his chair laughing when Dylan told his father about Angelina and her dad's shotgun.

"You were doing a story on Appalachian witchcraft?"

He nodded. "Yeah, but I didn't finish it."

"So this was the article that caused you to lose your job in Nashville."

Dylan stopped chewing and placed what was left of his burger on his plate.

"It was the story that caused me to *leave* my job, yes."

"May I ask why?"

Dylan decided to play it safe. "Because there was no concrete evidence besides what was already published in books down at the local library."

"And because you fell in love with the girl you were investigating."

"That, too."

Charles smirked, and Dylan decided it was time to change the subject before his reporter-dad started asking questions.

"So, what do you know about engagement rings?"

"Not much. Your mom's ring was just a simple gold band. It was all I could afford at the time. My other wives picked their own rings."

"That doesn't sound very romantic."

"I'm divorced, remember? Being romantic obviously isn't my strong suit."

Dylan grinned. "Do you think you'll ever marry again?"

"You never know. I'm still a relatively young man. I'm in good health. I did have a cancer scare last year, but it turned out to be a false alarm."

Dylan then told his dad about Celia and her cancer treatments.

"Angelina's been through a lot for such a young girl," Charles said. "Her dad's death. Her mom's cancer."

"Yeah, it's been hard on her, but she's strong. Really strong."

"I'd like to meet her someday."

"She'll probably insist on inviting you to the wedding. I don't want you to feel obligated to come, but—"

"I'd be honored to be there, son."

Son. Would he ever get used to hearing that?

Dylan quickly cleared his throat. "There won't be a wedding at all if I don't pick out a ring."

Charles laughed and tossed his napkin onto his plate. "True enough. Let's go find your girl a ring."

Dylan wasn't naturally an anxious person, but as he walked toward the pond, he couldn't ignore the trembling of his hands or the pounding of his heart.

It's not like she's going to say no. She proposed to you,

remember?

Angelina was sitting on the blanket with a sweater wrapped around her shoulders. The sun was beginning to dip below the mountains, and the light reflected on the water.

Dylan stopped walking and took a moment to just look at her.

He knew he could live to be a hundred years old, and he would never see anyone as beautiful. But it wasn't just her long black hair and bright blue eyes that stunned him. It was a thousand little things he knew would seem insignificant to anyone else. Her laugh. Her smile. The way she loved her mother. The way she adored her dog. The way she treated every single person who walked into her music shop as if they were her long-lost friend.

Dylan glanced across the water. Just along the edge of the maple trees was where their house would be. Angelina wanted two stories with a wrap-around porch facing the pond. They would live there. They would make babies there.

And they would grow old together there.

Angelina gazed at the mountains, smiling as she thought about her day. Their lives had been crazy lately, but today, she had actually taken the time to notice a calendar . . . and the date.

Never had a calendar made her so happy.

"You look so happy, sweetheart," Dylan said as she sat down on the grass. He leaned close and kissed her softly.

"I am happy."

"About anything in particular?"

Angelina grinned. "Maybe."

"Hmm. Keeping secrets from your fiancé?"

"Oh, I have many secrets."

"Well, it's a good thing I'll have the rest of my life to learn them all." Dylan played with a strand of her hair, twirling it around his finger. "Did you have a good day?"

She couldn't stop smiling. "I had a great day. What about you?"

"My day was . . . weird, but you'd be very proud of me. I spent the entire afternoon with my father."

"Is he still alive?"

"He was when I left him back at the office."

"Well, then, I *am* very proud of you."

Dylan laughed. "We had lunch and went shopping. It was . . . okay, I guess. It wasn't too awkward. I don't know that I could stomach it every day, but—"

"Wait. You went shopping with your father?"

Dylan nodded. "Believe it or not, he gave me some good advice. Since I had absolutely no idea what I was looking for, he told me to choose something that reminded me of you. And that's when I'd know."

"You'd know what?"

Dylan pulled the tiny velvet box out of his pocket and lifted the lid.

"I would know I'd found the perfect ring."

She blinked rapidly at the pretty ring nestled inside the box.

"Oh . . ."

Dylan removed the ring and slipped it on her finger.

"How did you know my size?"

"I called your mom from the jewelry store."

Angelina grinned. *Of course he did.*

"Do you like it? I know it's pretty simple. Just a single solitaire."

"I love it," she promised him.

The two of them smiled at the ring on her finger.

"So, what other magical charms are you hiding from me?" he asked.

"Hmm, well, I *do* have a secret to share."

Angelina's smile was beautiful as she leaned close and whispered in his ear.

Epilogue

"I can't believe she's thirteen," Dylan said, wrapping his arms around his wife's waist. Their front yard was filled with friends and family—and a lot of pink and silver balloons.

Allison Thomas loved anything girly and sparkly.

Dylan and Angelina watched from the porch while their daughter opened the last of her birthday gifts—a new guitar from her Grandma Celia and Grandpa David. She was surrounded by six of her best friends and her little brother, known among the girls as "the cutest six-year-old in the world."

"They're both growing up too fast," Angelina said, and Dylan murmured his agreement before pressing a soft kiss against her neck.

On the day they'd become engaged, Angelina had whispered in Dylan's ear that her period was twelve days late. This news led to a whirlwind trip to the pharmacy, followed by the longest three minutes of their lives.

Angelina and Dylan had married at the pond two weeks later.

Eight months after that, Allison Hope had arrived.

Just as her grandmother had predicted, Allison was blue-eyed and beautiful. From the age of three, it was obvious Allie was the opposite of her mom in that she was more than willing to embrace her supernatural gifts. Like her grandma, Allie had the ability to predict the future and had been the one to tell the family she had a little brother on the way long before Angelina even suspected she might have been pregnant.

As the son in the family, Caleb Michael Thomas missed out on cool things like magic spells and psychic abilities, but he was a constant source of happiness. Caleb was all boy and loved nothing more than wearing camouflage and fishing in the pond. His best friend was a beautiful chocolate lab named Petey. While he wasn't related to Cash—whom they'd buried nearly eight years ago—this dog was the spitting image of Angelina's childhood companion, and just as loyal.

Angelina sighed contently as she looked around at the smiling faces. It had taken more than a decade, but their family had finally found peace.

Grandchildren have a way of healing hearts.

Celia was sitting on one side of the picnic table, talking with Dylan's mom about their newest crafting project. Patti had moved to Knoxville soon after the birth of Allison, and she and Celia had become the best of friends. No one had cheered louder than Patti when Dr. Campbell had finally deemed Celia cancer-free and in full remission. When Patti wasn't busy teaching at the

University of Tennessee, she was in Maple Ridge, spending time with the grandkids and knitting with Celia. She had also stood by her best friend's side on the day Celia and David had exchanged wedding vows.

"Your dad's face is a little red," Angelina said, grinning at her husband.

Dylan smirked. "Probably talking politics with David."

On the other side of the picnic table was Charles Thomas, who was having a heated discussion with Angelina's stepfather about the upcoming governor's election. It had taken several years and many heated conversations, but Dylan had finally made peace with his dad. Charles had been retired from the paper for nearly five years, and no one had been more surprised than Dylan when his dad offered him the editor-in-chief position at the newspaper. He now lived in Gatlinburg and spent as much time in Maple Ridge as possible. Where he'd lacked as a father, he more than made up for it with his grandchildren. Charles loved nothing better than spending an afternoon with his grandson at the pond or sitting on the front porch while Allie played whichever instrument she "loved more than anything."

Allison was a musical prodigy, so the beloved instrument could change daily, depending on her mood.

Looking across the grass, Angelina smiled when her eyes settled on her best friend. Maddie was wiping strawberry frosting off the mouth of her toddler. Nick was in the yard, tossing a football to their ten-year-old. After he lost his job in Atlanta, Maddie and Nick had moved back to Maple Ridge. He was still trucking, and Maddie had returned to work at the music store.

"I know what you're thinking," Dylan whispered in her ear, making her tremble. "You want another baby, don't you?"

Angelina sighed. She couldn't deny it.

"Maybe one more."

Dylan nuzzled her neck, and she felt him smile against her skin.

"One more sounds good to me, but could it be a boy? I really don't know that I can handle another daughter turning thirteen."

Angelina laughed. Dylan had been dreading this birthday party since the day Allison had been born.

"The spell's not so bad. I wished for you, and now I have a happy and healthy family and two beautiful kids."

Dylan snuggled her close. "And a husband who can't keep his hands off you."

"That's nice, too," Angelina admitted with a grin.

As if she could hear their quiet conversation, Allison turned her attention away from her friends and gazed up at her parents standing on the porch. A brilliant smile stretched across her face, and Dylan sighed heavily.

Angelina bit her lip to keep from laughing. Dylan might have been dreading this day for thirteen years, but their daughter couldn't wait to blow out her candle.

"She's ready," Dylan said.

Angelina turned around in his arms. "What about you? Are you ready?"

"No, but at least she's not twenty-one. *That's* when I'll have a heart attack."

With a grin, Angelina raised herself on her tip-toes and kissed him gently.

Moments later, an excited Allie joined her parents on

the porch. She glanced over her shoulder and smiled at her grandmother, who was watching her with proud eyes. She then turned her attention back to her parents and reached for her father's hand. Dylan leaned down, and Allie sweetly pressed her lips to his cheek.

"I hope I'm as lucky as Mom," she whispered in his ear.

Allison Thomas gazed down at the shining candle. Its yellow flame flickered and glistened against the darkness of the living room. She had eagerly anticipated this day—her thirteenth birthday—since she'd been a little girl.

"Today is a special day," Angelina said, her voice solemn.

Growing up, Allie had heard the legend, which had been passed down from her mother. It was a fairy tale—much like Cinderella—but without the glass slipper or the wicked stepsisters. Instead, this story involved nothing but a shimmering candle and a simple song, both of which would allow the young girl to blossom into a strong and intelligent young woman. She would be beautiful and—at the age of twenty-one—would find her true love.

It couldn't be a fairy tale without true love.

From a young age, Allie had loved learning about her heritage, and her ability to predict the future had proven quite useful when it came to passing pop quizzes in math class. While some of her family's stories were crazy, not once had she doubted the story about the candle and the love charm. With long black hair and piercing blue eyes, her mother was stunning. Angelina Thomas was joyful, gifted, and wise, and her husband loved her as much today as he had on the day they'd married.

"Are you ready?" Angelina asked.

Allie nodded. Her heart was thundering and her hands were trembling, but her mother assured her this was to be expected. The ceremony was an important rite of passage in a daughter's life—a sacred ritual that had been passed down from her ancestors. One day, Allie would sit on the floor with her own daughter, and her daughter's candle.

"I'm ready," Allie said, her voice brave.

Her mother smiled proudly at her daughter as they joined hands. Between them, the candle danced, casting shadows upon the walls. Allie closed her eyes, took a deep breath, and began to sing.

> *"True love and sweet whispers*
> *Till death do us part;*
> *Send someone to love*
> *My Appalachian heart."*

Angelina gave her daughter's hand a reassuring squeeze, and with her eyes still tightly closed, Allison swiftly blew out the yellow flame.

About the Author

Sydney Logan writes heartfelt romances that feature strong women and the men who love them. In addition to her novels, she has penned several short stories and is a contributor to Chicken Soup for the Soul. She is a Netflix junkie, music lover, and a Vol for Life. Sydney and her husband make their home in beautiful East Tennessee.

Visit her online at www.sydneylogan.com.

Acknowledgments

This is the second edition of *Mountain Charm*. If you've read the book before, you'll notice it now has a new cover and a new publisher. I also fixed a few minor typos that we missed during the first printing. Beyond those changes, the book is exactly the same. If you're new to Angelina's story, I hope you love it as much as I do.

First and foremost, a special thank you to my readers. It's because of your encouragement that I felt confident enough to write this second book. Thank you for being so supportive.

Thank you to my editors—Wendy Depperschmidt, Shaina Hanson, and Elyse Evans. Also, thanks to Krista Richmond, Kathie Spitz, and JA Hensley for reading this manuscript in its earliest stages. All of you provided valuable advice and input, and I am forever grateful.

Special thanks to T.M. Franklin for designing the beautiful book cover for this second edition.

Finally, thank you to my husband for loving everything I write. I love you.

Matthew 6:21

Books by Sydney Logan

Appalachian Hearts Series
Lessons Learned
Mountain Charm
Soldier On
Stealing Hearts

Short & Sweet Collection
Cracks in the Crystal Ball
Meet Cute

Standalone Novels
Songbird
Listen to Your Heart
Turn the Page
Between the Raindrops

Novellas & Short Stories
Breathe Again
Once Upon a December
Force of Nature
Halfway to Anywhere
Winter Song

www.ingramcontent.com/pod-product-compliance
Lightning Source LLC
Chambersburg PA
CBHW021230130626
46554CB00004B/1421